The Ancient Medallion

D1714802

Nina Makhatadze

Nina Makhatadze

First printing

This book is a work of fiction. Names, characters, places, and incidents are the
product of the author's imagination or are used fictitiously. Any resemblance to
actual persons, living or dead, events, or locales, is entirely coincidental.

ISBN: 9798736551828

In loving memory of my parents,
Iosif Konstantinovich and Elizaveta Petrovna Makhatadze,
Also, in memory of my dear grandmother, Maria Alexandrovna.

Contents

Part One

Part Two

Part One

1 THE CALM

Judy was slowly walking along the water's edge of the warm Atlantic Ocean trying not to disturb the funny little birds swiftly mincing their tiny feet on wet sand. As if they were flirting with the great and calm evening ocean, they would gleefully chase receding waves for a little while, then come to a sudden halt, as if they were rethinking their actions and coming to their senses. Then they turn around, and all together run back escaping from the bounding water back to the shore.

Watching these unceasing little birds, Judy was dreaming about her new job and the astounding new career opportunities. Carried away by her thoughts, Judy did not notice that dusk was setting in and it was time to go back. One more time Judy glanced at the evening ocean and a white sail-boat lonely rocking on the waves faraway. Walking on the sand warmed by the sun during the day and passing by boisterous flocks of sea-gulls that had made themselves comfortable on the shore, Judy went to the boardwalk. She swiftly climbed up the stairs and found herself in front of a cozy restaurant. Judy looked inside the windows with curiosity. The restaurant was crowded and music was playing. At the open veranda there were white table-cloth covered tables on which candles flickered in the colored luminaries. Palm trees growing on the shore reached the open veranda, hugging it with their thick green branches. A fresh evening breeze was descending on the town, and everything seemed to be so temptingly inviting to come in, forget for a while your daily businesses and concerns, and spend a lovely evening.

At one of the tables, an animated group was noisily celebrating a birthday. A separate table held an elaborately decorated birthday cake with "Happy Birthday" on it written in chocolate. A dancing couple -- a gorgeous long-necked blond and an elegant handsome man -- was gracefully swinging to the music. Judy peered with interest at them. He was dressed in an immaculate dark suit; his moves were perfect. Growing grayish on his temples, his dark hair was neatly trimmed. His refined features and something confident and masterful in his appearance and manners gave him an irresistible gloss.

Judy smiled. She imagined at once scenes from her recent humorous novella where she had made herself a heroine. Mr. Balducci, the Stranger, Doctor Judy Green and their adventures – all flashed through her mind.

Inspired by the sea view, the music which she liked to listen in her car driving from the beach, and by the glowing prospects of her new job, Judy wrote a humorous novella where all incidents, characters, and places were fictitious and existed only in her imagination and where real people were transformed into heroes of her novella.

"Judy, hi," she heard a familiar voice. She turned toward the voice. An elderly man wearing a jacket and a baseball hat was approaching her leading on a leash a large dog with an elongated and delicate snout and a long reddish coat.

"Hi, Mr. Cornelli," she replied, "nice to see you."

"Jessy, Jessy, good girl," Judy reached to pat the dog on the head, exchanging a few pleasantries with her neighbor Mr. Cornelly. After that, they took a little walk on the boardwalk, chitchatting of one thing and another and enjoying the warm evening, the ocean view, and the setting sun.

Soon, however, Judy bid farewell to her neighbor and was driving back home. She had ahead of her pleasant arrangements to make for her upcoming moving to California and the beginning of her new job.

As usual, Kitty met her at the door with a warm greeting, digging her furry little face into Judy's leg, meowing friendly and following her around the house.

Being smart, Kitty sensed some upcoming changes in their life long ago and, of course, was eager to make her own contributions to their new venture.

2 THE ANCIENT TRUNK

Judy was going to complete her moving preparations as soon as possible to spend some time with her grandmother in Florida before beginning her new job. She packed everything essential in big boxes. Kitty made herself comfortable on the top of the great grandmother's ancient trunk and was closely and captiously watching preparations.

Judy planned to donate the trunk and some other belongings to the Salvation Army.

She tried to pull the trunk closer to the door; the weight of the trunk was completely out of proportion for its size and this always surprised her. However, since childhood Judy had liked this big wooden trunk with its metal fetters. It had been passed through generations in the family. She would settle down on the rug by the trunk, open it with a big carved metal key, and go through its contents: ancient clothes, coins, old photographs, and letters. She liked trying on dresses from the trunk and sometimes would dress up in them for the school carnivals or school literary gathering.

Judy could not resist looking inside the trunk one more time. She settled down by the trunk and as usual tried to turn the key in the keyhole to open it. This time, for some reason, the key would not turn and she could not open it no matter how hard she tried. Judy decided to leave it alone. "It's just a waste of time," she thought when all of a sudden something clicked inside the keyhole, the key turned, and the whole trunk started making strange squeaking noises. Frightened and surprised, Kitty leaped off of the trunk's top and stood up on her hind legs, dumbfounded to make out what was going on.

Judy raised the lid of the trunk, and watched astonished how the front side of the trunk, which has always seemed to be so massive, whole, and solid, split slowly in two, making a squeaking noise in the process and opening a chink between the splits. Judy froze on the spot with unexpected surprise and amazement. In the meantime, Kitty, who immediately tried to thrust her forepaw into the chink, brought Judy out of her light stupefaction.

Judy found her flashlight and held a light inside the chink. On the bottom of it she noticed a tiny object and tried to get it out. It turned out to be a push-button. Judy gingerly pushed the button. The bottom of the chink slid immediately apart, her hand dropped down and laid on some cold object. Judy tried to get it out and her efforts were successful.

Only now Judy realized that there was a secret compartment in her old great grandmother's ancient trunk of which she had never heard. Nobody in the family ever mentioned it, and, perhaps, nobody even knew about its existence. It seemed that the mechanism that hid the secret compartment in the trunk failed because of old age and revealed its contents.

Judy looked at the object she retrieved from the chink. It turned out to be an ancient Russian Orthodox icon the size of a rather small book. The whole icon was in a silver setting with small round openings through which heads of saints with golden halos in a shape of sun rays peeped through. The icon was placed in an elaborately carved box with a transparent top. In the right upper corner of the box were tiny angels, a shepherd boy and girl. The shepherd boy's hands were made up as if he was playing his tiny pipe, but the pipe was missing. She had never seen anything like this before.

Judy tried to open the box and have a closer look at the icon, but it was not possible to do so because the box seemed to be an all-in-one-piece.

Judy again thrusts her hand into the secret compartment. This time she retrieved papers yellowed by time, most probably letters, and some documents, and a big carved metal key, reminiscent of her trunk key and an object that instantly charmed her by its remarkable and extraordinary beauty. It was an ancient medallion on a chain. To be precise, it was half of the medallion. All colors of the rainbow were dazzling and glowing in this little wonder because it was completely and generously covered by sparkling stones.

The shape of the medallion was unusual; it looked like a heart split in two. Half of it was missing and on the split side were placed tiny red rubies; that sparkling, created the impression of dripping blood. Under the rubies, one could guess an arrangement created to unite with the missing part.

Judy could not take her eyes from this beauty. After admiring it for a while, she, nevertheless, put it aside and again fumbled in the secret compartment to make sure there was nothing else left in there. After that, Judy attentively looked through the papers.

The old letters were very warm and tender and were dated by the beginning of the 20th century. A touching story of two loving hearts torn apart by a tremendous force, but beating as one, bubbled in her imagination.

In her childhood, Judy liked to listen to her great grandmother's recollections about life in pre-revolutionary Russia and about some of her ancestors, relatives, and friends. What surprised Judy the most was that names mentioned in the letters were completely unknown to her. She strained her memory and tried to find some clue, but all in vain as nothing came out of it simply because she had never heard of them.

"Who were they, what relation did they have to her ancestors, and why had nobody ever mentioned this secret compartment?"

From her great grandmother, Judy knew that a rich collection of ancient icons was kept in her great great-grandfather's family. Unfortunately, most of these were lost during the revolution in Russia as well as the connections with many relatives and friends.

"What was so special about this particular icon, these letters, and the medallion, and why they were hidden in the secret compartment that nobody ever talked about?"

Strange finds excited her imagination and evoked her reflections that behind this thoroughly kept family secret, a dark mystery awaiting revelation could be concealed.

Judy carefully and attentively went through the papers and then packed them up neatly along with the icon and the key.

She decided to investigate their content more intently at a later time and continued with her packing.

Judy looked again at the medallion with admiration. It was an exquisite piece of jewelry and workmanship especially the tiny sparkling drops of ruby blood. Surrounded by such a touching romantic mystery and secrecy medallion, that at one time must have belonged to someone of her ancestors, emotionalized her and she eagerly put it on.

Meanwhile Kitty, this fluffy little "beasty" sitting in the trunk, where she got herself out of curiosity and, of course, of the desire to be an active participant of an event, watched the sparkling object with quiet and fond admiration and delight. She, just like her owner, apparently, was eager to find answers to many exciting questions and unravel the mystery of the ancient trunk and its enigmatic content.

3 THE TURNS OF FATE

***

Russia, Arkhangelsk Province. Beginning of the 20th century.

A Hard-Northern winter in the power of the rigorous Northern climate presents travelers with the sharp frost. It boisterously gambols with whirling snowflakes and the penetrating wind and ominously presages an approaching snowstorm. A trio of Orloff trotters melodically jingling bells and distinctly beating rhythm with their hoofs is rushing along the highroad in the midst of a thick forest trying desperately to thunder down the increasing noise. A sleigh, squeaking its runners on the frosty snow, follows it. In the sleigh a young Duke in rich clothes, shivering from time to time, is wrapping up in racoon fur.

Coachmen Phedorich, a stout and thickset peasant in a sheepskin coat, felt boots, and a fur hat urges the horses already weary, over heated by the fast ride.

"Oh dear, dear, don't let me down, don't let me down," the coachman keeps on saying giving one of the horses another whip.

Meanwhile darkness overpowers, the wailing of the snowstorm growing louder and louder and snowfall intensifies. The prospect of getting home today for the travelers becoming more and more unreal, and it looks like they are losing their way…

***

In the rich house of a prosperous northern business man, Alexander Varnavich Rechachev, and his beautiful wife, Praskoviya Artemievna, at Christmas Eve rein happy animation. Their children: charming daughters -- Anna, Maria, Klavdiya, Elizaveta, and son Alexander (Shurochka) are all engaged in the festive preparations.

The head of the house is a very respected statesman in the county and a Maecenas. He is an elected deputy of Russian State Duma, who dedicates considerable amounts of time and means to charities. Alexander Varnavich is also a notable healer in the county and successfully heals people with alternative herbal medicine.

There is a rich library in the house filled with multiple volumes where he likes to spend evenings studying ancient manuscripts. There in the library he keeps his violin – the work of one of the famous Italian makers. In his spare time, Alexander Varnavich likes to play his violin in the family ensemble with his daughters and son.

Alexander Varnavich travels a big deal over Russia because of the State and business matters and has just recently returned home.

The Children are enthusiastically decorating a beautiful Christmas tree, putting on it sparkling ornaments and sweets. Two elder daughters -- twins Anna and Maria are putting finishing touches on the beautiful cake they have created.

Meanwhile, five-year old Shurochka is trying to tease his sister, Elizaveta, a ten-year-old girl, bright and lively, and a splendid horseback rider, who is fondly attached to her young raven-black proud steed. She diminutively calls him Voroneiushko.

Shurochka hopped on his wooden toy horse and pretended to be a horse rider.

"Lizok, Lizok," cries he excitedly, waving his toy sabre.

"This is my Voroneiushko!"

Lizok (Elizaveta) in response aggrievedly purses her plush lips.

Happiness and children's laughter was filling up this light, warm, and prosperous house.

Meanwhile, outside the windows a violent storm is developing with the outburst of a raging tempest and a hard frost.

9

The next morning, however, was bright and glorious after the night snowstorm. Elizaveta woke up early, quickly got dressed and ran to the stables. She clenched a piece of sugar in the palm of her hand. Elizaveta approached her favorite black horse. The horse furiously shook his mane, snorted, and reared up onto his hind legs.

"Voroneiushko, Voroneiushko!" -- she called after him by diminutive. The horse heard her voice and surprisingly humbled down and bent his head. She opened her fist and extended him sugar caringly patting his mane. The horse with pleasure took the delicacy offered him. Elizaveta deftly mounted the proud steed, and soon the beautiful black horse and young girl raced across a dazzling snow-covered field. Her slightly narrowed, clear green eyes were full of excitement and admiration. Before long, however, the horse paused and became restive, pawing frozen ground, and rearing onto his hind legs. Elizaveta peered intently at a snow drift ahead. There she saw a turned upside-down sleigh and the horses nearby. She immediately surmised what could have happened there and rushed back to the village to call for help.

***

Judy completed all her moving preparations right on schedule. She had one week left before beginning her new job and had decided to spend it with her grandmother in Florida.

Just like Judy, grandma did not know anything about the secret compartment and its content and was equally surprised when she learned about it.

Together they tried painstakingly to shed some light on the dark family mystery, find some answers, or at least some leads to solve it. They went through the remnants of old letters, greeting cards, and old photographs that miraculously survived the turmoil of revolution and post-revolutionary soviet period, and were in their possession for years. They examined them with a magnifying glass in hopes that someone was wearing the medallion, or at least had mentioned it in the letter. All their efforts, however, were completely unsuccessful, they couldn't find out anything. Besides, born already after the revolution in Russia when the contacts with relatives and friends were long lost, grandmother knew little about her ancestors.

Time flew very quickly and Judy had to bid farewell to grandmother and leave for work. Nevertheless, she was full of determination to continue her search and investigations and unravel the mystery of her exciting finds.

She left for Los Angeles, where she had excellent prospects for her new job and career, leaving with her grandmother the old documents, letters, and the icon she found in the secret compartment. But the medallion, she instantly fell in love with, she put on and never parted with it. The big carved metal key she extracted from the trunk was inlaid with tiny grey stones and two small ivory human skulls and bones and was very unusual and elaborate. She decided to keep it, and symbolically called it "my key to solution."

4 THE NEW POSITION

Judy arrived at Los Angeles and joined the famous experimental group headed by the prominent Psychiatrist, Doctor Kristopher Van Bright. She had dreamt about this job for a long time. She had sent him a letter telling him about her immense desire and motivation to work with his team, about her love for the field and patients, her background, knowledge, experiences, and dedication. Doctor Van Bright had replied to the letter, invited her to Los Angeles and offered her a job.

His team was working on a very important scientific problem which implied a new approach for treatment of patients with especially severe forms of psychiatric conditions that were not responsive to conventional methods. His new approach could revolutionize the entire field of psychiatry. Under his supervision there was created a new installation, by means of which the effect of medicine selectively was magnified in certain centers of the human brain, that let physicians significantly reduce general treatment dose and avoid undesirable serious and severe side effects of treatment. It was the first step for the selective brain centers oriented targeted treatment and prevention of many severe psychiatric conditions.

For these works, Doctor Van Bright has been nominated for a prestigious international scientific award.

His team also participated in a large-scale research and treatment of patients with impulse control disorders. Patients were offered comprehensive treatment and observation in the hospital and clinic.

Some of Judy's long-time patients from her previous job agreed to participate in the study, were admitted on treatment and arrived with her at Los Angeles.

Her hard and persistent work with patients and research publications; communications with more experienced colleagues -- all let her quickly and effectively elevate her professional level and acquire the knowledge and self-confidence so needed in her new job.

Judy, entirely submerged into the whirlpool of her daily hospital activities and research, for a while forgot about her recent exciting findings in the trunk.

Judy's workday in the hospital started as usual with a morning conference. Right after the conference she went to the ward to see her new patient. She approached the ward and knocked on the open door. Her patient -- a man in a grey hospital robe was sitting motionless and stared with unseeing eyes at the window.

"Mr. McRae, I am Doctor Green," Judy appealed to the patient.

"I would like to talk with you."

The patient would not move and did not reply to her greeting.

Unexpectedly, Judy overcame with some strange feelings. The silhouette of the patient reminded her of someone; she definitely had seen him before, but where?

Judy got closer to the patient and looked in his face. Immediately her heart sank, she could not utter a word. Pausing for a little while, Judy tried to start conversation again, but in vain she did not get any response. Her patient remained completely impassive.

"Well," she said "if you are not inclined to talk to me now, I will drop in later."

Judy blushed up to the roots of her reddish hair and went out. She got her breath back, she recognized him. It cannot be a mistake she thought. That's him, that elegant man from the cozy restaurant at the seashore is now sitting in his grey hospital robe in the psychiatric ward. A man, whom Judy called in her heart the Stranger and who became a prototype of the hero of her humorous novella.

Judy fixed her eyes on his chart. His name, age, and diagnosis, that seared her heart -- everything was now under her hand.

For a moment she imagined that cozy restaurant, the dancing couple gracefully swinging to the music, the Stranger. However, Judy quickly got back to reality. Mr. Stranger or Steven McRae was sitting motionlessly in her ward. He is seriously sick, and unfortunately, his sickness does not always easily respond to treatment.

Judy had to continue her rounds and see other patients. She had some urgent matters to attend: to prepare her report for the day conference, see the results of investigations and patients' treatment, give new orders, conduct conferences with patients' relatives and friends, prepare discharge papers -- in general complete her usual routine of daily hospital activity.

As the day progressed, however, Judy was able to talk to Mr. McRae and gather all the necessary information, conduct detailed physical and neurological examination, and intently investigate all his previous laboratory works, medications and their results.

"Well," she mused with sadness,

"It looks, after all, our acquittance took place."

She finally got to her office and sat in her comfortable chair.

"Now," she thought, "the quality of his future life to a considerable extent will depend on my abilities and skills, and on the efficacy of my treatment." Her tasks were not simple.

First of all, she needed to win his trust and regards, achieve his awareness, acknowledgement, and understanding of his malady, which is possible and necessary to fight. Understanding occurring gradually and slowly, going hand in hand with effective treatment. He should feel the support of his doctors, relatives, and friends, feel that he is not alone with his disease, that doctors, relatives, and friends are all on his side. Judy needed to make him her ally in the fight for his health and return to full-bodied life, and she threw herself into the fight.

Judy straight away made changes in his medications, ordered him new laboratory investigations and planned conferences with his relatives and friends.

Day by day she watched her patient. Her persistent energetic measures were not without positive results. To her pride and satisfaction, the patient slowly, but surely started improving.

5 JANNETTE

Judy parked her new Honda, which she lovingly called my Gray Mouse because of the gray color and the perfectly streamlined shape. She swiftly reached the elevator. She was in a hurry because she had to see new patients in the clinic with Doctor Van Bright and students and by no means did she want to be late. Before the encounter she attentively looked through the chart of Mrs. Jannette Swenson, a hundred-year-old patient who suffered from the mild form of the hypochondriac syndrome.

Recently, Mrs. Jannette lost her husband of many years and she felt keenly for her loss. Her bereavement lingered on and got complicated with depression.

"Well, it's quite a worthy age," Judy took a note knocking on the door and entering the room.

As soon as the patient saw Judy, she burst out crying.

"Oh, doctor, I'm so sick, so sick, so, so sick!" she kept sobbing, complaining, and moaning slightly shaking her blond curls. Her big, still beautiful aquamarine-blue eyes were full of sadness, hopelessness, and despair.

Judy extended her a box of tissue and let her vent. After that, she talked to her.

Jannette was overwhelmed with her grief. She'd lost her husband of many years, and with him any interest in life. She constantly was thinking of death.

Judy evaluated her condition and decided to hospitalize her as she was suicidal and needed medications and psychotherapy as well. Jannette agreed.

After that, Judy saw a few more patients and along with Doctor Van Bright and students, participated in teleconsultation of patients from other hospitals. Her workday was winding down and she went back to the wards.

Not without satisfaction and delight, she noted that things were going very well, and patients were improving.

She bade farewell to everybody and soon left the hospital for the club. An important addition to patients' treatment with medications and psychotherapy was broad involvement of them to social life and amateur activity, which bore the character of patients' social rehabilitation, especially those whom disease deprived habitual social connections and doomed to loneliness. For this reason, on the initiative of Doctor Van Bright and with financial contribution of his relatives and friends -- renowned actors, artists, and sportsmen, many of whom were former patients of his, the hospital purchased a big and spacious house where the club activities were held.

Everybody was fond of the club and lovingly called it simply "Our House."

Trees and well-tended gardens with flower-beds and arbors surrounded the house. Everything was suggestive of comfort and care.

Among the patients undergoing treatment at the psychiatric department there were professional actors, musicians and sportsmen. With their help, Doctor Van Bright first created an experimental theatre troupe and musical ensemble. The club became the center of social activity in the hospital. At the evenings there were conducted joint games, and on the holidays, festive meals. Nobody felt left behind and everybody would contribute whatever they could. Doctor Van Bright himself participated in the stagings. He beautifully played several musical instruments, was an excellent dancer, and possessed a good sense of humor.

Everybody realized the importance of their contribution no matter how small or large it was. The charitable performances of the experimental troupe were so popular that they would be invited to perform in other towns and even states.

The psychiatric department, headed by Doctor Van Bright and his experimental group, were well-known nationwide not only because of the theater troupe, but also because of the excellent results of the patients' treatments.

6 THE "INSEPARABLE FOUR"

A charitable event of a great importance for the hospital was to be held in the club house with participation of the theatre troupe, and Judy had some ideas about it. She wanted to share them with her friends, who were long time patients of hers.

There were ongoing preparations for a dress rehearsal in the club…

"Stop, stop," she heard the producer's voice when walking toward the buffet and passing by the hall. Her attention was attracted to a group of people marching the corridor in a dignified manner. Leading the march was Suzi, an elderly and a very round lady pushing forward her walker. On the walker, she had neatly stacked piles of newspapers, magazines, books and a purse. Behind her, as usual, followed Napoleon, short man of approximately the same age, then Miss Azelia Pincus, a lady of undetermined age inclined to put on weight, painstakingly trying to keep balance on her high heels. She was frequently adjusting her hairdo slightly jerking her shoulder in the process. A tall, bearded, and slightly round-shouldered man by the name of Robinson finalized the procession. The Inseparable Four, as everybody called them marched to the Bingo hall where the game was going to start shortly, and comfortably settled at one of the bingo tables.

"What are the cards saying today, Suzi?" Napoleon asked, looking at her inquiringly.

Suzi meaningfully rolled up sleeves of her blouse and took out of the purse one of the numerous packs of cards. She customarily laid out cards on the table with her small, white, plump hands bringing close to her lips a beautiful ring in S shape with a large sparkling stone. At that, Suzi giggled softly and glanced at Napoleon with her small, dark and naughty eyes.

"It looks like tomorrow we're gonna have a hot day!" Suzi replied weightily.

Meantime, Judy passed to the buffet, took a menu, and looked attentively through it making some notes in her tablet.

"Well, I guess it's time to do it as in the old days!" Judy mused and immediately recollections surfaced in her mind. She imagined a little red head girl in an apron; she had dark, swampy green eyes and a huge bow on her head. The girl was zealously whipping eggs for her sponge cake. After a while she anxiously examined her cake, which to her surprise, for some reason more resembled scramble eggs.

"Don't you worry, dear," mother said to her, "try it again and you will certainly get it right."

The little girl had a huge sweet tooth and very much liked cookies and cakes and for that reason she had been experimenting with baking since her childhood. Baking became one of the passions of her life. Year after year she would collect recipes of all kinds of cookies, pastries and cakes. She would work on them, modify them, bring them to perfection, and create new ones. With great pleasure, she would entertain her relatives and friends with her baked goods, and the habit became an integral part of her nature.

Judy got an idea to use her baking talent and immense culinary experience for the charitable event and organize an exhibition-sale of her baked goods.

An ample kitchen in the club house with refrigerators, oven, stove and other equipment perfectly suited her intentions. She needed help to recruit some volunteers among patient's relatives and friends, who had experience in handling public food.

Judy looked for the Inseparable Four. She found them in the Bingo hall. The game had not started yet, so she had a few minutes to talk to them about her plan, which was met with enthusiasm.

"We'll help," proclaimed Napoleon with animation, immediately assuming a leadership role in himself.

Earlier, Judy had discussed the matter with Dr. Van Bright. He too liked the idea. Now Judy needed to outline her menu, make a list of all the ingredients she will need for her baking and much more. She decided to get down to the business without a delay.

Finally, Judy got home. She opened her mailbox, which she had not checked in a couple of days. She immediately noticed a large blue envelope with an ancient post stamp and an ornate handwriting. She opened the envelope and started reading. It turned out to be an invitation for dinner, which will be held on Vampire Street, house number 666, and the signature read "Dracula."

The envelope and its content were quite unusual, but Judy did not make much out of it assuming that it was most probably an invitation to one of the home theatres or simply a joke. She put the envelope into her purse and soon forgot all about it.

The next day, as usual she started her workday with a round of her patients. Things were going very well. Results of the intense work using the latest research innovations and technology were impressive. Patients were steadily improving. Mr. McRae or simply Ray as everybody called him, was getting much better. Slight deviations from his normal thinking were immediately detected by a special experimental device and relayed on a computer monitor. All the necessary measures were employed immediately not to permit the full-blown psychosis to develop. As the matter of fact, his condition improved so significantly that a decision had been made to discharge him for outpatient treatment, which included psychotherapy.

As Judy completed her teleconsultation and psychotherapy session, she got back to the wards. She wanted to round her patients one more time before biding everybody goodbye.

On Jannette's night stand she noticed a pile of books. Judy walked up to the stand, opened one of the books and started reading: "His strong hands were passionately squeezing and caressing her round buttocks. Her hips opened for a hug winding around his shapely body. Their lips amalgamated and became one in a hot extended kiss taking them to an exciting world of sensuality and bodily pleasure. Devouringly his tongue slid over her breast and nipples. The pleasure bordering with pain spread over her entire rather small and resilient body straining it and trying to free it from fetters of the persistent penetration. Their breath was becoming more frequent. Faster, faster, one more moment and a sweet moan, almost a cry was heard in the semi darkness of flickering candles...."

Judy closed the book and opened another one. She looked through book after book to find out that the contents of them were very similar.

"Well, it's quite a selection of literature for someone of a worthy age," Judy mused with a smile. "The good thing is she's got her interests back."

One week passed after Ray's discharge and Judy, with an understandable excitement, was looking forward to their first outpatient session of psychotherapy.

The intense day in the hospital wound down. A rehearsal with Dr. Van Bright was scheduled for today in the club. They were going to play piano a quatre mains and, of course, Judy did not want to be late. She left the hospital and headed to the club right away. She parked her car and swiftly got to the entrance. To her surprise, the club door was locked and a hanging sign stated that because of the repairs in the club house it's temporarily closed and all the rehearsals will be held in another location. There were fliers with the exact driving directions on how to get there.

"Oh, that's so nice of them," Judy mused, taking one of the fliers. She got back to her car and started the ignition. For some reason her navigator stumbled, and she happily used the flier.

The driving directions were very detailed and precise, so she found her destination easily.

7 THE VAMPIRE BALL

Sparkling with its metals and slightly squinting eyes-headlights, Gray Mouse drove up to the house number 666 on Vampire Street.

It was a big, two-story mansion overlooking the ocean and surrounded by beautiful gardens.

"Nice house," Judy made a note, "more resembles a castle, but the lighting is rather dim. Probably costume rehearsal has already started."

"The Vampire Street number 666, is an interesting name, something familiar."

"Of course," she recalled her strange blue envelope.

"Well, it looks like someone is trying a practical joke with me," flashed through her mind and she confidently walked up to the entrance and opened the door.

Before she even entered the house, two men dressed as vampires approached her. One of them held out his hand and plainly pronounced: "Your telephone, iPad, and watch, please."

Judy pulled out of her purse her telephone, iPad and along with her watch, handed it to a vampire. Only now in the dim light of the big hall she noticed people sitting on the chairs. They had tapes on their mouths and their hands were tied in the back. Judy even did not have a chance to get astonished when she heard Ray's slightly husky voice:

"What was that noise coming from the garden yesterday?"

"Mr. Dracula," one of the vampires replied, "a couple of dudes tried to get into the house."

"Oh, yeah, where are they now?" with unconcealed irony asked Ray.

"Well, for now in the refrigerator and then…."

Judy grew pale, blood slithered out of her face, and she staggered. At the same time, one of the "vampires" approached her and she recognized him as Ray.

He was dressed in some strange black tights, a white shirt jabot, and black high shoes with laces. His outfit was supplemented by a black cloak and a scarlet band on his neck. His hair grew up slightly and curled up on his temples.

Judy refused to believe her eyes and ears. She, nevertheless, composed herself, and tried to give her voice confidence and firmness.

"Hi, Ray," -- she pronounced as usual as she did in the hospital.

"My name is Dracula; I want you to know." Judy bit her lip.

"Mr. Dracula, what are you going to do with these people?" she asked trying to hide her emotions.

"Well, we're ready to have dinner with guys," he replied with dignity.

The chill sent up Judy's spine and red spots started to appear on her face. She fully realized that she had to do something and act urgently, but how?

Her mind was feverishly working.

"What really are their intentions, what are they going to do?"

Judy tried to talk to Ray again.

"Ra…" -- she stopped short, "Mr. Dracula, I want to talk with you," but Ray would not let her continue.

"Doctor Green, you can make yourself comfortable in your room. You will be seen at dinner and, please, do not forget to change your clothes for dinner. You will find everything you need in your room."

Accompanied by two vampires, Judy went up the wide staircase and passed to "her room." Vampires remained outside behind the door.

In the room, she immediately dashed to the window, drew away the heavy curtain, and tried to open the window. It would not give way and seemed to be glued. Besides, it was too high to jump from to the ground.

Judy looked out of the window and the view opened before her eyes: the night ocean and the full moon as if it was sliding over a glimmering moon pass.

She strained her eyes and noticed dark figures calmly rocking on the waves. Suddenly the dark figures mounted their surfing boards.

There was something ominous in their coordinated moves resembling a dance and in their black costumes glimmering in the moonlight. On their foreheads small lanterns were radiating soft blue light.

Judy put back the curtain and moved away from the window. She was tormented by her thoughts. When and how had she made a mistake? What did she overlook? How could all these things possibly happen? She was doing her best and had surrounded her patient with motherly care. Everything was thoroughly thought over, all aspects of his treatment and return to a full body life. Multiple consultations were carried out with the patient's relatives and friends. He slowly, but surely, had responded to treatment and his condition was improving steadily. She was so happy about it. Now, because of her apparent failure, innocent people can be hurt.

Dispirited, Judy absentmindedly looked around. She saw a huge, old-fashioned bed, on which an ancient dress was laid, probably her outfit for dinner. It was a fair place with ancient candlesticks and candles, a few ancient chairs, a polished folding table with wheels, an easy chair, and a couch.

Oh yes, she has to change for dinner. At this moment, someone knocked on the door.

"One moment, please," Judy replied. She hurriedly put on the dress, which surprisingly fitted her perfectly, and opened the door. At the threshold stood a woman vampire dressed in blue exotic eastern clothes. Her long jet-black hair was spread over her shoulders. She was holding in her hands big and sharp scissors. Judy became alarmed and prepared for the worst.

"My name is Neila," she pronounced with a self-complacent smile slightly grinning and showing off her snow-white fangs.

"Follow me," she said courtly leading the way, slightly swinging her round "as full moon" hips in the process.

Judy followed her. They went through a dimly lit passage to a small room that looked like a hairdresser's shop.

Neila settled Judy into the chair and lifted scissors to her face. Judy's entire body strained, but she remained motionless. The vampire woman cut off a few hairs of her forehead and made her a pretentious hairdo. After that, Judy was accompanied by two vampires to a dimly lit dining room, where a table was laid with a snow-white tablecloth and silver. In the middle of the table, there was a huge silver plate framed with an inlaid rim with engraved thorns. The plate was filled up with dark sea pebbles and black-gray sea sand in which tiny flickering torches were scattered. In the center of the plate there was a tiny fountain with bubbling scarlet liquid that reminded Judy of blood. In the dim lighting of the flickering torches, the sensation that the thorns were continuously crawling out of the plate has been created.

"Oh, sure, a little bloody fountain in the middle of the table to increase a vampire's appetite, an appetizer, so to say," with sadness Judy tried to make a joke.

On the fireplace there was a big metal grayish-brown boat-shaped plate also filled with the same pebbles and sand, in which tiny torches were flickering.

Shortly, Ray appeared. He approached her and invited her to the table. Judy agreed and took her seat at the table. The vampires served a delicious dinner, filled glasses with red vine, and retired.

The dinner went peacefully and quietly. Tired and hungry after her workday at the hospital, Judy had some food and wine and started to feel a little bit better, but the thoughts about innocent people who could be hurt did not abandon her. A few times she caught his eyes on her medallion, with which she never parted, but which had always been covered by her clothes. The ancient dress with its low neck exposed it. Even under the dim lighting of the dining room, her medallion was sparkling and glittering in all its dazzling beauty, not mentioning the streaming "blood drops."

After dinner a soft clavichord music started playing, and Ray invited her to dance. Judy agreed, because there was nothing else, she could do at the moment.

During their slow dance, she felt his breathing on her open shoulder and his fangs slightly touching her neck skin. Judy was trembling like an aspen leaf whether of fear or the proximity of his breath, she couldn't say.

Finally, the music stopped, he thanked her for the dance, and the two vampires reappeared to see her back to "her room."

Judy was exhausted, and once in the room, she laid down on the bed without getting undressed and fell into a deep sleep.

She, probably, slept quite a long time.

When she woke up, she looked anxiously around touching her neck, pulse, hands, legs – fortunately everything was in place.

She got out of bed, walked up to the door and listened. It was very quiet in the house. She opened the door and did not find the "vampires" behind it. Judy cautiously went through the corridor and down the stairs. The house was absolutely empty. Dracula, the vampires, and the hostages -- all had disappeared.

"Where did they go?" Judy mused. She found the kitchen and walked up to the huge refrigerator. Anxiously and with trembling hands she opened it. It was completely empty, only two plastic rabbits rested lonely on the shelf. Judy closed the refrigerator and went out of the kitchen. On one of the chairs in the big hall, she found her watch, telephone, and iPad. She grabbed them and hurried out of the house.

Her Gray Mouse was safe and sound, and in the same place where she had left it yesterday. Judy got into her car and started the engine. Surprisingly, now the name of the streets did not coincide with her driving directions and she turned on her navigator. This time, the navigator worked perfectly and she reached her hospital very soon. Getting out of her car, she lifted the skirt of her ancient dress which she had not changed, wanting not to linger in the "vampires" house. She rushed to the elevator and squeezed herself into the closing door.

"Hi, Judy," she heard a familiar voice. "You did not show up for the rehearsal yesterday. We were worrying about you; what happened, are you okay? By the way, that beautiful dress you're wearing looks very nice on you. Where did you get it?" The rest Judy did not hear. She just collapsed to the elevator's floor and was ready to cry as if she were a child.

At last, Judy got up from the floor and went to her office. There she changed to the hospital uniform, calmed down, and was ready for work. But before that she wanted to clarify something. She started calling to Ray's relatives and friends with whom she had communicated during his treatment in the hospital. To her surprise, all the telephones turned out to be out of service. Judy tried to talk to her coworkers, but nobody knew anything about repairs in the club house. On the contrary, all rehearsals went smoothly and uneventfully.

Judy fell into a muse: "What was that, was it a dream? Why has everything related to Ray disappear without a trace?" She simply couldn't comprehend what had happened to her.

"Who are you really, Mr. Stranger, Steven McRae, Dracula, or simply Ray, as everybody called you? Are you some kind of werewolf or what?" sluggishly she tried to make a joke.

Nevertheless, Judy had urgent matters to attend. On her work table there were piles of papers -- charts, graphs, research papers, all laid out. She was getting ready for her upcoming conference and presentation on an International Meeting of Psychiatrists in Paris. Their trip to Paris with Doctor Van Bright and other colleagues would be held in a few days, and Judy needed to concentrate entirely on her work, and forget, at least for a while, about her recent shocking experiences.

8 THE MONK

The workday at the hospital was winding down. Judy came back to her office and one more time looked through the papers spread on her table. With a sense of content, she gathered them up into the folder. All preparations for her departure to the Conference were completed. Kitty had been set up with a pet sitter, and Judy was looking forward to an exciting trip to Paris.

Her flight to Paris was uneventful. Judy, along with Doctor van Bright and other colleagues from the hospital, departed right on time and arrived in Paris exactly on schedule. They reached the Hotel, where the International Conference of Psychiatrists was to be held, in the late afternoon and, hence, were able to attend the registration and the traditional meeting of colleagues and friends. The official opening of the Conference and beginning of the work was scheduled for the next morning.

After the opening, Doctor Van Bright's presentation on a plenary session was such a great success that it evoked interest not only of the Conference, but also of the media. He acknowledged the good work and contribution of his team and during a television interview was surrounded by a group of his coworkers including Judy.

The intense work of the Conference, as usual, was combined with cultural measures, parties, and seeing the sites of the City of Lights, not to mention meetings arranged by private companies, where latest technologies were presented in a relaxed atmosphere.

The fine weather held in Paris, and the summer evening was warm and clear. Two friends were absorbed in a conversation as they leisurely walked down the street. They went to a café and customarily made themselves comfortable by the table.

"Hey, Etienne, what would you drink?" the friend asked him as a waiter approached.

A tall handsome guy, Etienne with curly and slightly reddish hair, keenly eyed the TV screen and seemed to be stirred.

"Are you okay?" anxiously inquired his friend, tracing his gaze and noticing that Etienne all of a sudden grew pale.

On the TV screen meanwhile, Doctor Van Bright, surrounded by his coworkers, was answering reporter's questions.

"Yes, yes, sure, everything's fine," replied Etienne absently.

The program of the day came to a conclusion and Judy had some free time to enjoy. She left the hotel and went strolling down nicely kept paved streets and viewing shop windows. Along the way, she liked watching her reflection in the shop windows and with pleasure would examine herself from head to foot.

Judy crossed the street and glanced at the shop window again. Something evoked her attention. A silhouette. It seemed that she had seen it already several times, but where? Oh, of course, on the opposite side of the street.

"Well, it looks like I have a fellow-traveler," flashed through her mind.

Judy continued her walk, but after a while she suddenly stopped and turned her head. A tall young fellow wearing a beret, under which slightly reddish curls stood out, immediately looked the other way and hastily wandered off. Judy paused to think; "Is it just a coincidence or is someone really following me?"

Well, she did not make much of it anyway. She went to a nearby café, got herself an ice-cream, returned to the hotel, and soon forgot all about it.

The next day she planned to visit Notre Dame de Paris.

Judy walked up to the cathedral, located in the heart of the city, and with great interest and curiosity was inspecting this magnificent construction.

Its perfect towers, the spire, the stained-glass windows, the main façade, and the sculptural panel over the Portals – all of it she tried anxiously to fix in her memory. She also made a few photographs and entered one of the heavy doors, decorated with forged reliefs.

She found herself in the huge semi-darkened hall with pillars.

There was a service going on and the cathedral was crowded. Unlike the hall, the high altar was well lit up. Judy needed some time to get used to a dim lightning to move freely and not bump into multiple visitors.

A tall, dark figure moved away from one of the pillars and slowly started approaching Judy. He was completely wrapped up in a dark cloak and resembled a monk. His face was hidden in the hood and couldn't be seen. The monk approached Judy, came to a halt and froze in front of her for a moment. Judy somehow came to feel that he fixed his eyes on her medallion. What happened next was completely unbelievable and Judy was ready to faint. The monk slightly opened his cloak and something gleamed on his chest. Judy did not believe her eyes.

"Medallion! A sparkling medallion with a little 'stream of blood!'" It was her medallion, or a very similar one!

"Is it possible or am I dreaming?"

These exciting questions Judy was asking herself not a first time in a comparatively short period of time.

Judy did not even have time to recover from her amazement, as the monk wrapped himself in a cloak again and disappeared mingled with other visitors.

Not realizing what she was really doing, Judy chased after the monk, trying to catch up with him. She ran out of the cathedral to the street and stopped for a moment to look around and catch her breath. At this very instant she felt on her neck somebody's long, thin, and tenacious fingers. She did not immediately perceive what was happening. One moment and the medallion would be torn off her neck and lost forever! What happened next was completely unimaginable and unbelievable. With a strong kick, someone knocked down the thief who did not have a chance to finish his job. With the agility of an acrobat, the thief instantly got back to his feet and fled the scene.

Completely stupefied and bewildered, Judy stood in front of the cathedral clutching her medallion in hand. The whole episode was so quick and ephemerous that surely could be taken by on-lookers as some kind of theatrical performance.

Shaken, Judy returned to the Hotel. She took a shower, had something to eat, and lay down on the huge bed. She started to cast about in her mind, as in slow motion, step by step, everything that had happened to her during the day.

So many questions are now crowded in her mind.

"Who is this monk, is he really a monk, and if not, who is he?

"Where did he get his medallion, how did he find out about her medallion, and what he was trying to tell her demonstrating his medallion?

"Who tried to tear off her medallion, and who knocked down the thief, and prevented the robbery?" -- All these and many other questions and thoughts did not let her rest.

Judy took off her medallion and started attentively examining it. As far as she noticed it, the monk's medallion was very similar, but still, something was different about it.

"Of course!" it struck Judy. "His medallion, or part of the medallion, was like a mirror reflection of hers, which could mean that he's got her missing part!

Does it really mean that on that monk's neck there was the missing part of her medallion?"

"Well, the further the better," she mused: the more she thinks about it, the more complicated it gets.

It looked now that "surprises" and shocks had become inherent companions of her life.

In spite of all the happenings and unanswered questions that had poured on her in the last few days, Judy decided do not linger in Paris. After completion of the Conference, she would return home along with their group. Her patients and Kitty were waiting for her, and, besides, a charity event was fast approaching and she had all the intentions to use her culinary abilities. Nevertheless, thoughts about the monk and his medallion firmly lodged in her mind.

"Looking for the monk in Paris, is the same as looking for a needle in a haystack, unless he himself comes forward again," thought Judy.

Along with Doctor Van Bright and other colleagues, Judy boarded the flight and soon the airplane took off.

Trying not to be seen, two strangers at the airport were watching her departure from the distance.

"Boarding is over; she is leaving," said one of them.

"She will be back," his companion assured him.

9 MR. CENTAURIES ALPHEUS –
THE AMATEUR ASTRONOMER

The last few months for Judy were full of unexpected surprises and shocks, which she slowly was getting used to. In the airplane she had some time to think over all these happenings.

"Will the monk become some kind of a key to help her solve the puzzles, and is there really any connection between them? Is the monk's medallion virtually a missing part of her medallion, and if so, where and how did he obtain it?"

She found hers in the secret compartment of the trunk that belonged to her family for generations and was thoroughly and successfully hidden from everybody for over a century. What relation could possibly exist between them?

"Why did he demonstrate his medallion. Was it a message for her? and if so, what had he wished to say, what was his aspiration, and how was she going to find a needle in a haystack?"

All these questions tumbling about in her mind gave her no rest and evoked her meditations. "It looks like unraveling this mystery will not be an easy task," she concluded.

On their return from the Conference, a warm reception has been held in the hospital for the participants with many congratulations for their successes and well wishes for new achievements. The future for Judy seemed to be so promising and exciting.

At the same time, the charitable event was fast approaching, and preparations for the cookout were set in full swing.

After getting all her daily things done at the hospital, Judy set off to the club house to meet with the Inseparable Four and discuss with them some practical matters about the cookout.

She drove up to the club house and once inside the hall, she started looking for them, and suddenly overheard an interesting conversation

"Napoleon, she is the woman of my dreams, but unfortunately I do not have even a slightest hope."

"Not a slightest hope?" – with a tinge of doubt repeated Napoleon.

"Yes, not the slightest hope. She is a woman of Society!"

"A woman of Society?" – echoed Napoleon.

"Yes, the Society. The SOCIETY OVER 100. They admit there only people who have reached a mature age – of 100 years and older, and I can assure you their rules are very strict!"

Unwittingly and with understandable curiosity, Judy traced Robinson's gaze.

Having made herself comfortable by the table, with crossed legs and leaning back on the chair was sitting Jannette. She was wearing checked black-blue-white slacks, a blue cardigan, a white shirt, and blue shoes with white socks. She coquettishly waved her open blue fan with a golden floral design, slightly shaking her golden curls in the process. Her huge, still beautiful aquamarine-blue eyes, were intently watching the popular television quizzing game, the Slippery Road. With totally incredible ease and agility she was giving correct answers to all the questions, evoking well deserved delight and admiration of those around her. Her broad erudition and preserved keenness of mentality were impressive! Judy couldn't help but admire her herself.

Meanwhile, Judy approached the table of the Inseparable Four. Suzi, as usually, was spreading out cards with her small, white, plump hands, customarily bringing close to her lips the beautiful ring in S shape with a large sparkling stone.

"Hi, Doctor Green, how things are going?" Judy was greeted by them.

"Very well," she replied, taking her seat by the table.

The Inseparable Four, with Napoleon as their leader, briefed her on recruiting the volunteers, while she was at the Conference in Paris.

"Good job and a good team," Judy remarked when Napoleon finished.

All the volunteers recruited had an experience in the handling of public food and now, Judy thought everything will depend on how well they virtually fulfill their project.

After her conversation with the Inseparable Four, Judy returned to the hospital for her night shift in the ER.

Upon her arrival Judy consulted a few patients in the ER parlor and was entering her orders and recommendations into the computer.

"Doctor Green, you have new patient," she heard over the intercom. Judy saved her data, stood up and went to look for her new patient.

"Hi, Mr. Sikkimor, I am Dr. Green. It's nice to meet you," customarily she introduced herself, casting an intent evaluating glance over the patient in the process. The patient meantime would not take his eyes from the TV screen. He was very agitated and preoccupied.

The multi-lingual and multi-vocal "choir" of the media and the public expressed deep concerns and preoccupation with an impending new serious threat on Earth. On everybody's mind and tongue were words – black holes, black tube, Galaxies, collision....

Mr. Andrew Sikkimor, whom everybody called Centauries Alpheus (hinting to the Alpha Centauri system), – was a middle-aged man, tall, lean, blue-eyed, and hook-nosed. He constantly was adjusting round glasses on his nose bridge. His wavy light brown hair, growing grey on his temples, desperately needed a haircut.

For several nights already, he tirelessly and without a wink of sleep could not tear himself from his telescope. During the day after the sleepless nights, he would feverishly check his charts, maps, distances, and calculations.

"Will they succeed, will they do it on time?" He kept muttering, and restlessly stirring put up under the chin his long, thin fingers.

Before his eyes a marvelous picture was opening: a spacious hall, walls of which represented a giant computer screen. On the screen a breath-taking picture was developing with the Universe and shining stars.

Three Galaxies are drawing closer to one another. Two of these elliptic, supermassive galaxies are approaching the Milky Way. The Galaxies start changing their contours exposing black holes and releasing Jets. The black holes unite and form a gigantic black tube. The small and beautiful blue planet in the solar system, Earth, is under grave threat. The entire Milky Way Galaxy is under the threat. In case of the Galaxies collision, the planet Earth and the whole solar system will be consumed by the black tube. Impending catastrophe seemed to be inevitable.

In the middle of this gigantic hall with facing computer monitors are sitting captains of the constellation of Captains. They are arranged and situated in a way that imitates the outlines of their constellation. They are dressed in golden and silver outfits that radiate a soft light, the color of which corresponds to the color of their stars. On their heads they are wearing personal computers, the shape of which resembles the spiral Galaxy "Veronicas Hair." By means of "Veronica's Hair" all the pertinent captains' thoughts were collected, concentrated, and directed to the major computer "Superior Intellect." The "Superior Intellect" would analyze the data and give the best engineering decision.

Each captain wears a necklace, that symbolizes the unity of their planets. Each necklace consists of rare and most precious rocks of the planets of their constellation. The "Assembly of Captains" were held on special important Galaxy occasions. Because of the grave danger to the Solar system and the beautiful planet, Earth, captains were assembled to save the Milky Way from imminent demise.

In front of each captain there was a control panel. They were watching happenings on the monitor of the gigantic computer. Using the energy of stars, they created a protective power sheath around the Milky Way to push away approaching two super galaxies. Mr. Centauries Alpheus, as a representative of the planet Earth, was also sitting in front of the control panel and, of course, on his head he too, had Veronika's Hair.

Between the Captains and the Superior Intellect, dialog was constantly kept. They were verifying astronomical distances, energy of protective sheath, changing galaxy configurations and other important decisive matters.

On the monitor screen, a critical moment finally developed and the countdown started in the anticipation of the collision. ... Three, two, one ... and in an instant a bright light-radiance and a general rejoicing filled in the hall. Victory! Brilliant engineering decision has worked. The Galaxies started separating from each other, the black holes coiled up and the black tube disappeared. The collision was avoided and the Earth was safe!

"Mr. Sikkimor how did you sleep last night?" Mrs. Gladys Williams, the nurse of the psychiatric ward, asked the patient.

"Where am I?" casting incomprehensive glance around asked the patient.

"You are in the hospital, Mr. Sikkimor. Yesterday in the ER you were very sick, and Doctor Green decided to hospitalize you."

The Nurse gave him medicine, checked his pulse, blood pressure, explained to him the daily routine, and advised him to get dressed and have a walk in the inner garden of the ward.

Mr. Andrew Sikkimor, a former computer engineer and an amateur astronomer, had recently lost his favorite job at a very prestigious high-tech company because of research discrepancies with executives. He insisted on his research point of view which was not completely understood or shared by them. Because of this he decided to dedicate all his time and stringent efforts to astronomical investigations and save planet Earth from the impeding catastrophe....

10 THE EVENING OF SURPRISES

In the early morning before the charitable event, the bakers' team gathered in the club house kitchen and was getting ready for work.

All teammates were wearing white aprons, white caps, and white T-shirts with an inscription saying: "The First Annual Exhibition-Sale of Baked Goods by chef Dr. Judy Green."

With much animation and enthusiasm, bakers rolled up their sleeves and got down to business.

A few hours later they produced a wide variety of marvelous baked goods: cookies, cakes, cupcakes, bars, buns, and breads. All the baking was immediately packed up, labeled and put on a nice display. They gave eye catching and romantic names to their cakes like: The Unforgettable, The Masterpiece, The President, Napoleon, Josephine, The Ideal and others. Finally, all the work was completed and with much delight and excitement, they could admire the results of their efforts.

With a few minutes left before the beginning of the show, the audience started filling up the hall. The event was very well advertised in the media and all tickets were sold well in advance.

In the hall, there were tablecloth-covered tables with coffee and the baked goods where the public could taste them and if desired make purchases in the buffet.

The bell rang announcing the beginning of the show.

"Pirate's Joy" a play by a young and yet unknown playwriter, and a former patient of Doctor Van Bright, had at the beginning evoked many objections, but finally was approved and accepted for production.

Judy completed all the necessary preparations and went to the hall, where the show was already playing. On the stage two pirates -- a woman and a man in a hot fight -- were inflicting painful blows. Amidst their fight, all of a sudden, the woman pirate has stopped and meekly bended her head.

"You won, Horatio. I loved you all these years, from the moment I first saw your portrait and clung to it with my lips."

"My portrait!?" almost choked Horatio.

"Yes, Horatio, look" and she pulled out a piece of a neatly folded old paper, hidden on her bosom. She handed it to him. Amazed Horatio took the paper in one hand while adjusting his black mustaches with the other and looked at it. On the paper there was a drawing, under which sign stated:

"Wanted, pirate by the name Horatio…"

"Do you remember, Horatio, when the police first started looking for you? Your portraits, then, were hanging everywhere!"

Horatio swallowed his saliva.

"Then why do you always fight me, Fiona?"

"I am jealous, Horatio, jealous of everything I could never be equal to you!"

"Oh, yeah, and what is that?" He asked with a barely perceptible doubt in his voice.

"It's your stupidity, Horatio," she replied, giving him an unexpected crushing blow.

The first act was over, and the audience burst out into applause. During intermission, everybody could taste coffee and cookies and purchase them in the buffet.

The success of the evening exceeded all expectations. The public was very content and gave the actors hot applause. The Exhibition-Sale of the baked goods evoked enormous interest because of their amazing taste, freshness, and attractive looks. All the cookouts were sold out. Judy

40

immediately got invitations to participate in the Food shows that were held in the town on a regular basis.

There was quite an animation of excitement, and congratulations after the show. A good sum of money was collected, too. All proceeds were intended to be used for purchasing of new costumes and decorations for the theatre and for improvements in the club house.

"Hey, Hector, come down from that ship. You are not really going to take a long voyage on her, are you?"

"No, you won't sail too far, that's for sure" – pirates joking and laughing were heard. At this very moment something fell from the decorations with a horrible bang, and the exaltation gives way to bewilderment as everybody runs back to the stage.

Hector was laying on the stage face down with a knife sticking out of his back. Everybody froze with horror. Doctor Van Bright, dressed as a leader pirate, Morgan, with a black patch on his eye, a wooden leg, and a big talking parrot on his shoulder, Abraham, first got to the body. He checked his pulse on the carotid artery and declared, "Dead."

A blood-curdling shriek from Abraham suddenly brought everybody out of stupor.

"La haem, la haem, la haem..." cried he. His cry was suddenly drowned in a fierce fire alarm shrill, meaning that all of them immediately had to leave the building by the special outlined beforehand route.

Everything happened so quickly and so unexpectedly.

Test alarms had been conducted in the hospital and in the club house all the time and everybody was familiar with it and for this reason the building has been vacated in an organized fashion, quickly and without panic. Soon police and firefighters arrived. They checked thoroughly the building, and not finding anything wrong declared a false alarm. But when everybody returned to the stage, a new surprise was waiting for them. Hector's body has disappeared without a trace. Police and detectives immediately started an investigation and witness questioning.

It was already late night, or early morning when Judy returned home. But in a few hours, she had to be back to the hospital.

The next day everybody in the department, of course, was dispirited and disappointed that such a successful event ended up in a total failure.

However, their surprises were not over yet!

In the wards appeared a man, wearing the hospital uniform, who caused them a complete state of shock. He was walking down the corridor in his new crisp snow-white sneakers with a barely perceptible guilty expression on his face.

"Hector, is that you!?" he was asked cautiously and with a hint of some surprise and consternation.

"Sure, it's me, what's up?"

"What's up, what do you mean what's up! How do you feel, are you okay?"

"I feel fine, why? It's just, I regret, I missed yesterday's show. I was dead tired after my night shift and overslept. This never happened to me before, and I can assure you it will never happen again" ....

11 BEARS, BEARS, BEARS

It's been one year already since Judy moved to Los Angeles from the town on the East Coast of the Atlantic Ocean, Our Bear Garden.

The year was saturated with many events and exciting impressions in her life. The persistent work to improve herself let Judy significantly elevate her professional level and now she was ready to sum up her accomplishments.

Along with Judy were a few patients of hers that had moved to Los Angeles to undergo experimental treatment in the psychiatric department headed by Doctor Kristopher Van Bright.

Judy was returning to Our Bear Garden to take part in the annual Psychiatric Research Conference.

She liked this town, located where two wide rivers unite. Belted with modern bridges and overpasses, the town represented a distinguished combination of new and old that blended harmoniously to each other. It's Grand Marina with a multitude of white yachts looking as sea gulls rocking on the waves, an ancient palace, XVIII century buildings, parks and, of course, bears -- all make a memorable impression and give the town its special coloring. Passing through the town, travelers immediately realize why it's called Our Bear Garden. Because there are bears there, many of them. Bear statues in full height and dimensions, dressed according to the impeccable bear taste, made themselves comfortable in the town parks, streets, in front of shops, buildings and businesses. Furthermore, the town was getting ready for the Grand Jubilee – the tricentennial celebration of its foundation and because of it, the bear "population" in the town was increasing daily according to the mathematical progression.

The Research Conference coincided with the tricentennial celebrations and for this reason Suzi and Napoleon, who were the natives of Our Bear Garden declared that they would not miss such an important event in their hometown for the world and were coming along with Judy.

The airplane in the local airport landed right on time. An interesting group of tourists disembarked the plane. Leading the march was an elderly and a very round lady lively pushing a walker in front of her. Of course, it was Suzi. After her, followed a curly blond with aquamarine-blue eyes was Jannette, slightly leaning on Judy's arm. Next to her, Mrs. Azelia Pincus was painstakingly trying to keep her balance on her high heels frequently adjusting her hairdo and slightly jerking her shoulder in the process. Behind them, Napoleon – a short man, and a tall bearded and slightly round-shouldered, Robinson.

Tourists were excitedly talking to each other. They discussed an amusement program that had been offered to them. They stepped out of the building where a minivan was already waiting for them. Soon they all made themselves comfortable in the van and drove to a large rental house by the sea.

The ample house with comfortable furniture, elevators, cozy bedrooms, grand covered veranda, a well-equipped kitchen, amusement areas, and a swimming pool were simply amazing and everybody liked it. There was an ocean view in front of them. The evening breeze, and the sounds of surf had a very beneficial effect on everybody and let them forget the long flight tiredness. However, there was an intense program ahead and they needed good rest.

On the morning after their arrival, Judy was very busy and could not take part along with the others in seeing the sights of the town, taking photographs with bears for the club house, and visiting the famous Farmer's Market. The Market which because of its unique goods and coloring was not only an important commercial center, but also a downtown tradition, where friends could meet and socialize with each other, where people could meet and talk to anchors of local TV and Radio stations, and to functionaries of the City, especially during elections.

Judy was going to join the party in the evening in her favorite restaurant by the beach.

She woke up in the morning, made herself coffee and went out to the veranda, where only sounds of the surf and seagulls disturbed the silence. Rising out of the horizon, the sun warmly caressed skin, instead of burning it with its hot bright rays. Judy finished her coffee and went down to the garage and soon she was driving along the highway in one of their rental cars.

Throughout the day she had exciting meetings with her friends and colleagues, interesting presentations, and patient counseling. She did not even notice how quickly time flew away and her workday wound down.

12 AT THE RESTAURANT

Light-footed on her high heels, Judy entered the restaurant wearing a dark blue, almost black, open dress that outlined her tiny waist. Her long, voluminous, and wavy hair glowed with natural golden red glitter and winded round her neck and shoulders. Two large black pearls gleamed mysteriously in her ears and reflected the depth of her dark eyes that contrasted pleasantly with her white, slightly pinkish complexion.

Entering the hall, she halted for a moment to cast a glance at the dancing couples. Before long, the music changed, and the public began lining up for line dances. Judy joined them and they all began dancing enthusiastically. Suddenly she paused and turned around.

"Ray," she called after a man who happened to dance some little distance away. The man elevated his eyebrows in surprise and with an air of astonishment made her feel that she was taking him for someone else.

"So, he's not Ray," she thought as blood gushed to her head thickly turning her face red.

"Whoever he is, they look very much alike."

At that moment, Judy overcame with the insurmountable desire to hold his gaze on her and she singled herself out and started to dance. Her whole resilient body was wriggling and rolling gracefully to the music, which she loved and felt finely.

At last, the music stopped, and the dance was over. Judy glanced round looking for the man, and their eyes met. At that, slightly raising her chin and somewhat tilting her head sideways, that gave her an air of challenge, she looked him straight in the eyes.

His face, however, remained completely "impenetrable" and calm.

"Judy, here you are," Azelia called after her.

"We are looking for you."

Soon a waiter approached her and asked politely,

"A party of six, Mrs. Green?"

"Yes, please," she replied.

"This way, please," he said and led them to the veranda.

The party was assembled. They ordered their meals and in anticipation of dinner were exchanging their photographs, recollections, and impressions of the exciting day. The delicious meal, the pleasant music, and dances made their evening. They all felt very happy.

At last, the gay party left the restaurant. Suzi and Napoleon decided to take a walk on the beach and the rest of the party hopped into the van and drove off home.

The weather began to change, and it seemed as if it was going to rain. The ozone smell filled the air and the great and severe ocean demonstrating its power and strength again and again, was crushing huge waves to the shore breaking them pitilessly down into the foam that crawled immediately back to the deep. It was growing dark, and a few tourists walked leisurely on the deserted beach lighting their way with flashlights. Two dark figures approached an elaborate sand castle with two big sand turtles ensconced nearby. The figures paused for a while to admire the castle and the turtles.

"Napoleon," said one of the figures, "I want to talk with you."

"Sure, Suzi, I listen," and he brought her plump little hand to his lips. Suzi gleamed at him with her dark, naughty eyes.

"Napoleon, I thought over everything. I want Billy," she blurted out.

"You want Billy?" The revelation struck him dumb, crushed on him as thunder in a clear sunny day.

"Yes, Napoleon, I want Billy and only him!"

"Well, after all, it's her right to choose Billy over me," he mused with sadness.

"Napoleon, he is so cute, so romantic!"

"So cute, so romantic," absentmindedly repeated Napoleon.

"He's got such little trousers!"

"Little trousers?"

"Oh, yes, yes, such little trousers, and a carrot in it!"

"And a wh..at, in his tro…u…sers?" asked Napoleon, stuttering.

"Carrot, carrot, carrot!"

"A carrot in his trousers? Suzi, are you sure about your choice?" asked Napoleon looking in her eyes with unconcealed pain.

"Oh, Napoleon, you took it all wrong, I need Billy from the Farmer's Square."

"Billy from the Farmer's Square?" astonished Napoleon "Billy, the bear, the statue of the Farmer's Bear!?" Napoleon exclaimed, not believing his ears.

"Yes, yes, yes, him!"

"Suzi, why do you need the statue and what are you going to do with it?" Napoleon implored anticipating big troubles ahead. However, Suzi did not listen to him, and his words seemed to hang frozen in the air.

"I need your help," she declared firmly.

One has to mention that Suzi and Napoleon were longtime friends and oftentimes helped each other in certain "worldly" situations.

13 THE MARATHON

It was a bright Sunday morning, but over the unruffled surface of the water the light morning mist was still hanging. At the start point on the broad river embankment, the marathon participants were gathering in some small, animated, and cheerful groups.

The marathon and the bicycle race under the banner "Run with Us, Roll Your Wheels, and Improve Your Health," were conducted for the Research Conference participants as well as for the locals as health improving measures, and were very popular among both. To secure the uninterrupted races, some downtown roads and bridges were detoured. Neither the engrossed race participants nor their onlookers really noticed when and how Farmer's Bear Billy got swaddled in a gray thick fabric completely hiding him from the observation. There was a sign saying: *"We are sorry, the statue of Billy is temporarily not available for observation because of the restoration works. Reopening of the statue will be held next Thursday (right after the rain), and the date...."*

When after a couple of days curious officials could not find out who was conducting the restoration works, under whose authority, and why it was that the brand-new statue needed restoration, they decided to uncover it before the stated date. To their great disappointment, they found that the statue was gone! Instead of Billy, there was a wooden ladder, masterfully camouflaged as the bear. The supposition was made immediately that because the statue was located in the Farmer's Square in the vicinity

49

of the Farmer's Market, where the big trucks were not a rarity at all, the statue could be moved away on one of them.

Billy was literally "screwed" away in plain sight along with a rather small pedestal, heavy bolts that screwed the statue to the pedestal, and the polite sign that so kindly provided the useful information. The questions, however, who and why had stolen Farmer's Bear Billy, dressed in some little blue trousers, checked red-white shirt, red polka dot handkerchief and a little bundle of carrots in his pocket, remained completely unanswered.

The disappearance of Billy naturally startled the whole town, especially kids, who loved taking pictures with their favorite beast, and, hence, rumors about its disappearance immediately spread throughout the town.

Suzi left the beach and went back to her bedroom. On her coffee table there was her iPhone, which she had forgotten to take with her to the beach. She took the iPhone and started intently listening to her messages.

"Hi, come down to the appointed place, same time. I need to talk with you."

Suzi put the telephone in her purse and went down to the garage leaving her walker behind. She drove to town and soon was approaching a large building by the river. Part of the building facing the road served as a shop where beds, mattresses, and other home utensils were sold. The back side of the building stretched toward the river bank and was used as a warehouse. There, on the river bank, was an arbour completely surrounded by shrubs, and a small pier with a boat fastened to it, slightly rocking on the waves.

Dusk was gathering, and two figures were approaching an arbour from two opposite sides: a heavy set and very rounded elderly woman, surprisingly agile for her age and weight, and a rather short man of approximately the same age. He was limping and breathing heavily. They both got inside the arbour.

"Hi, Suzi, how are you?"

"Hi, Gruben, I am fine."

"Let me get straight down to business, Suzi. You know, I had always highly appreciated your 'professional qualities,' as you are one of a kind who can steal the moon from the sky in a plain sight, and, at the same time, convince everybody that it had never even been there!"

While talking, he slightly loosened his bandana, and immediately something gleamed on his neck. It was Gruben's famous moving tattoo. A snake crawling around his neck, which had one green and one yellow gleaming eye.

"Oh, Gruben, come on, you definitely overestimate my abilities."

"Suzi, where is the beast?"

"Beast, what beast?" Suzi seemed to be surprised.

"You know what beast, where is the bear from the Farmer's Square?"

"The bear? I don't understand." Silence followed.

"I came here with a group. We are going to start a new business; I do not know anything about your bear."

"Suzi, I hope that's true; this time it is very serious, I warn you!"

One has to mention that Suzi has got deeply stung in her "professional" feelings. Right under her nose someone had stolen her favorite statue, to which she already boiled up with all her soul. Who else besides her could possibly pull this out so successfully? Not only did her "professional" feelings suffer, but also her curiosity and she firmly became determined to find it out.

The next evening, after her conversation with Gruben on the veranda of their rental house, Suzi customarily spread out on the table one of her multiple packs of cards.

"Napoleon, do you remember that case when precious paintings were stolen from the Mega Yacht?" That case had outraged not only Our Bear Garden, but the whole country as well. An audacious robbery had been committed in spite of the thick security and protection. The paintings are still missing. That time, I remember, Gruben had served as the chief of security and was a witness of the robbery. But still, they accused him of negligence. Besides him there was another witness, whose name has never been learned. That time they couldn't find any evidence against him. The security company that was in charge of protecting paintings insisted that the names and the facts were not going to be disclosed to the public until the investigation was over. To regain their reputation, they decided to find the paintings themselves and return them to the museum. But the paintings have never been recovered and I am just dying to find out that witness's name. Surely, Gruben would not share this information with me. I remember, though, the lawyer who represented Gruben that time was a famous one from the "Do not Judge Severely" law firm. Suzi cast her swift lightning-like and meaningful gaze at Napoleon.

14 THE LAW FIRM
DO NOT JUDGE SEVERELY

The Law Firm Do Not Judge Severely was situated downtown. Over the entrance was a sign that read: "The Law Firm Do Not Judge Severely. Two Brothers, Mr. Root and Mr. Chestnut, are always at your service." And, of course, two friendly bears at the entrance were more than glad to embrace you in their beary arms and invite you to visit their firm.

After the cordially beary clasp, customers dive into an atmosphere of high professionality, prosperity, and hospitality.

In a cozy and comfortable hall, the floor was covered with soft, deep, and fluffy rugs. Customers were sitting on the leather sofas and arm chairs; the stands and coffee tables were full of new magazines, cookies, and refreshments. On a grand TV screen information for customers featuring the work of the firm was displayed, and in a large aquarium a goldfish and many other exotic fishes were swimming.

Knock, knock, knock – two elderly men have just crossed the hall, one after the other exactly keeping in step, synchronously knocking their canes, and casting their swift and penetrating eyes over the customers.

A well-nourished lady in high heels carrying a small red purse under her arm while desperately trying to keep her balance, approached a receptionist. She frequently was adjusting her hairdo, slightly jerking her arm in the process.

"What's your name, Mrs., and how can I help you today?" she was asked politely.

"Oh, darling, you see, my name is Azalea Pincus, but everybody calls me simply Azelia. It's an unusual name, don't you think?" she said slightly rocking on her heels and without waiting for reply, continued rapidly speaking:

"Oh, my god, such a pretty dress you're wearing, it looks so very nice on you. Just where did you get it? You see, my dearest late mother loved flowers, and, particularly Azaleas so much that she called all her eight daughters Azaleas: Azalea Albus, Azalea Pincus, Azalea Flavus, Azalea..." and she was counting fingers on her palm one by one.

"Mrs. Azalea, how can I help you?" said the receptionist, desperately trying to steer the conversation in the right direction.

In that very moment, one of the customers, Mrs. Jannette Swenson, who came in for speeding, driving with expired license, and an indecent offensive gesture to a police officer, suddenly grew pale and she was clutching the left part of her chest. Drops of cold sweat appeared on her forehead and it looked like she was writhing with pain.

"I am so sick, so sick, so, so sick!" clacked she, shaking her blond curls and rolling her eyes expressively.

The customers and the personnel likewise reacted and set into motion immediately. They called for an ambulance, but the situation got even more complicated when on one of the leather arm chairs, someone noticed a strange packet that did not belong to anybody in the hall. The alarm was set off and before police arrival, everybody immediately left the building.

During the well understandable confusion in the firm, two people slipped into one of the rooms unnoticed, apparently losing their way out. A plump and round lady very dexterously got to one of the file cabinets, opened it and deftly went through papers pausing for a split minute on one of them.

"Okay, good," she said, "let's go."

Police and an ambulance arrived without a delay. Mrs. Jannette was placed into the local emergency department. The package turned out to be completely innocent, one of the distracted customers simply had forgotten all about it.

Judy was delightfully rocking on the waves watching in amusement the countless schools of fish coming her way with the flowing waves. It seemed to her that in an instant she could catch the fish and grab them into her bare arms, but with an incredible and completely incomprehensible precision and speed, the schools would change their direction, pass her by without touching her, and swim away.

"How do they do that?" she was wandering leisurely.

Now and then some of the fish would jump playfully out of the water, and wriggling in the air, gleaming with their silver scales before diving back.

Judy got out of the water and idly laid down on the warm sand covering her face with the towel. Now, she just wanted to forget about everything in the world, even about that new interesting book, she was reading on her tablet, and she began slowly dozing off. Her telephone rang.

"Yes, sure," muttered she, "something necessarily should happen." By the time she dug out the cell phone from her bag, it had stopped ringing. Judy looked through her messages; there were three of them.

"Doctor Green, this is Robinson, Jannette is in the hospital; she's had a heart attack."

Judy immediately got up, gathered all her things and literally flew into the house. She changed and rushed to the hospital. She found Jannette in the Emergency department. Napoleon, Suzi, Robinson, and Azelia were by her side. Judy looked at the monitor. Her EKG and other indicators were not immediately alarming.

"How do you feel, Jannette," Judy asked her, intently watching her face.

"I am fine now and can go home," she replied with a smile.

"Oh no, of course not. This is completely out of the question," but Jannette insisted. She also refused any other investigations offered her by Dr. Topkins. All Judy could do is to keep her in the hospital for observation for a few days.

Two fishermen with fishing poles in a small boat were casting off the pier, located near the warehouse.

"Gruben, have you talked to her?"

"Yes, I have," he replied.

"And, what does she say?"

"She denies any involvement in the theft."

"Do you believe her?"

"I don't know; I did not expect her confession at any rate. We have to watch."

The "holidays" by the sea were soon over and it was time to go back to Los Angeles. But Judy still had some unfinished business to attend. She was going to visit her precious nieces and nephews -- a younger generation of the family. The University, where the reunion was supposed to take place, was not far from Our Bear Garden and Judy couldn't miss the opportunity of meeting them.

In a grand and brightly lit sports hall of the University, severe black costumes and colorful outfits of partner dancers were flashing to sounds of Latin rhythms. The competitors danced with grand animation, passion, and enthusiasm. Judges were strolling in between pairs, keenly watching their every move and making some notes. Judy could not take her eyes from one of the couples, admiring their bearing, grace, and skills. Two curly red-heads are her nephew Joseph and niece Maria. They both were enthusiastic music lovers and ballroom dancers that made Judy very proud of them. To support their cousins, youth came from the other states. After the competition, they all together went to the restaurant and had a lovely evening. She was very proud of all of them, especially of their enthusiasm, future prospects, and plans. At that time Judy did not know yet what a significant part each of them would play in the staggering and dangerous adventures that were in store for her.

Jannette was discharged from the hospital and she surprisingly was feeling very well. She even rejected an idea of a wheelchair and insisted that she would make it easily to Los Angeles.

At last, all the preparations were completed, and the party was ready to depart. In the same van they arrived in the airport, and, in spite of Jannete's hot resistance, put her into the wheelchair. They did not have to wait long. Soon boarding was over and the airplane took off.

15 THE SHOCK

Being an avid golf player, Doctor Van Bright was regular in the golf club. After the game, two fellows of approximately 60-65 years old, made themselves comfortable in the club café. The inscription on their shorts was proudly stating: "Better Than Golf Can Be Only Heaven." They ordered some coffee and pastry.

"Listen Warren, I am telling you bindingly that the guy was dad, I checked it myself."

"Are you sure about that?"

"Absolutely. I do not have even the faintest doubt."

"You know, practical jokes are not such a rarity among the actors. When did it all happen?"

"A week ago,"

"What about police?"

"Well, the police are questioning witnesses and conducting thorough investigations, but the body disappeared, and Hector turned out to be alive, which complicates the matter. An audacious crime had been committed in a plain sight and a more audacious attempt to cover it up. Something is going on in the hospital. I feel it, some kind of underwater current which I know nothing about. I do not rule out the idea that some well-organized group of criminals is behind it. I am most certainly determined to find it out!"

They finished their breakfast. A smiling waiter approached them and asked politely,

"Is everything alright, can I get you anything else?"

"No, no, thanks," they both replied.

Warren got up from the table first. An unkind vicious green light unnoticed by Dr. van Bright gleamed in his eyes. They paid for the breakfast and left the café.

The airplane with tourists landed safely in Los Angeles. Jannette, as promised, made her trip without complications. Change of climate, and two-weeks' rest by the warm sea, had a beneficial effect on everybody. In the airport they parted. Napoleon and Robinson were seeing Jannette, Suzi, and Azelia, while Judy found her Gray Mouse in the parking lot and drove off home. On her way home, she stopped to pick up some groceries and Kitty from her pet sitter. It was late when she drove up to her house. Kitty, being impatient, was angrily scratching in her cage. Judy walked up to the door. She suddenly was overcome with some unexplainable alarming feeling. Judy opened the door and looked inside. To say that she got just struck dumb at the sight in front of her means to say nothing at all. She became frozen out of horror on the threshold. The house was a total mess. Everything was upside down; all drawers were hauled out and the contents were scattered on the floor. Horrified by the sight, she was ready to sit on the floor and cry. Judy plunged into the armchair. It took her a while before she could compose herself and walk through the rooms. Surprisingly, nothing was stolen and yet, someone had been in her house looking for something. "But what, what were they looking for?" Subconsciously, her hand reached to her medallion; it was in place.

Judy took pictures of the disorder and helplessly sank back into the armchair. She acutely and desperately needed to talk to somebody and share her frustration. What came to her mind first was to talk to Doctor Van Bright to whom she felt not only grand respect and gratitude, but also an immense trust.

The next morning Judy went back to work. Coworkers were glad to see her. She could not talk to Doctor Van Bright because he was out of town for a few days, so she had some time to think over her decision.

At the club house things were returning to normal, but police were still questioning witnesses trying to learn every single detail of that ill-fated evening. The Inseparable Four plus Jannette, as they were called now, were regulars at the club, because they liked playing cards and Bingo, and immensely enjoyed each other's company. At first sight, everything seemed to be back to normal, and their life returning to its usual course, and yet, something was different. Some silent knowledge and understanding between them, some secret that only they shared. At that time, Judy did not have an idea that a similar "search" was conducted in their houses too.

Because of the new circumstances, thoughts about the medallion and its mystery now firmly stuck in her brain, and she decided to return to Paris and try to find that monk. Again, and again she would recall all the details of her Paris trip trying to find something to get hold of. The "Shadow," that followed her on Montmartre – was it by chance occurrence, or had someone really followed her, and if so, who was he, and for what reason?

In a few days, Doctor Van Bright returned to Los Angeles and she called him on his home phone and asked whether she could drop in and talk with him.

"Oh, sure," he responded immediately.

Doctor Van Bright's villa was situated in a green picturesque neighborhood with the flower beds all around the house. Doctor Van Bright invited her to the study and offered her some coffee and refreshments.

"How are things going, Judy. How did you like the conference?" he inquired.

"It was good, in general, besides the incident with Jannette, which turned out to be not too bad." Judy told him all about their scare with Jannette. She hesitated. She did not know how to switch their conversation to her disturbing topic.

"Doctor Van Bright, is there any news about the police investigations?"

"No, not that I know of."

Lingering for a while, Judy finally uttered.

"Doctor Van Bright, there was an act of vandalism in my house. When I came home from the conference, the house was a complete mess, everything was upside down; it seemed as if someone was looking for something, but surprisingly, nothing had been stolen."

Doctor Van Bright listened to her with extreme attention.

"Any idea, what they could have been looking for?"

"I do not know. Maybe," Judy replied. Then she told him all about her mysterious trunk and finds. After that she handed him her medallion, and he attentively looked at it.

"Beautiful thing," he said thoughtfully.

"What are you going to do? Did you notify the Police?"

"No," replied Judy.

"First, I would like to find that monk and talk to him."

"Do you realize that this may be an extremely dangerous thing to do."

"I don't know. Maybe, but that's what I think I have to do."

"Well, at least keep me informed."

Doctor Van Bright showed genuine interest in her story and offered his help and support if needed. Judy accepted it with gratitude.

16 THE PARCEL

Russia, Arkhangelsk Province. Beginning of the 20th century.

***

A grand northern river, a giant fettered by ice is trying to release itself from the shackles and take a deep breath with its whole wide bosom. Spring is in the air and a thaw is just settling in. A hard-northern nature slowly and unhurriedly is waking up from a deep and prolonged sleep.

A girl on a raven-black horse is rushing across the woods to the river. Dusk is setting in and the night promises to be foggy. Occasionally, small animals frightenedly cross her path leaving their footprints in the snow, or some broken off twigs creakingly whirl down from the trees. She daringly advances forward on her black horse not paying attention to any forest noises around her. At last, she approaches the river bank, dismounts her horse, and tethers it to a tree trunk. Now one could see that she is caringly snuggling something to her chest. She gets on the ice and continues her way on a snow across the frozen river. The sky is overcast and not a single star, nor the moon would light up her way through the clouds. She is in a hurry and runs as fast as she can.

"Quicker, quicker, quicker. I have to make it. I've got to make it." Blood is throbbing at her temples. She runs without looking down or watching her steps. The snowflakes are blinding her eyes and she narrows them up. She knows there is a small islet ahead, and she hopes to get some rest there.

All of a sudden, black clouds clear up, and the moonlight shines from the sky lighting up her way. At that very moment, something mysterious and unexplainable makes her stop, and she opens her eyes and looks down. What she sees makes her blood freeze in her vessels with horror. One instant, one more step forward, and she would be engulfed and taken under the ice by seething water in an unfrozen gap. She caught her breath, carefully avoided the gap and continued her run. She reached the islet, but it looks like she can't rest, she can't lose time; the ice is ominously cracking under her feet, and at any moment can give way and crush succumbing to the immense destructive force. There was ahead still another smaller river to cross, that already was cleared of ice. On the farther bank of that river, a boatman happened to notice the girl. He immediately untied his boat and rowing vigorously, swiftly reached the islet. He put the girl with her parcel in the boat, and safely crossed the river. They had barely gotten out of the boat and stepped on the brink, as the ice on the great river broke and moved with immense thunder and force, and the entire islet that had seemed to be so safe and reliable a shelter, in an instant was completely engulfed and covered with water and ice. The girl was saved.

***

Judy was going back to Paris. Of course, she had some business there to attend, but her main reason was to get on the monk's track. How she was going to do it, she did not have any idea. What should she do to find someone she didn't even know in a multimillion city? Apparently, the spirit of an adventurer was concealed in her, and for some reason, she believed she would succeed.

The silhouette that had followed her on Montmartre and she airily did not pay much attention to, now seemed to have some mysterious meaning. On her arrival to Paris, she took the same hotel, and decided to repeat the roots of her daily strolls as on her previous visit.

She left her hotel and walked up toward Montmartre, admiring in the process paintings and pantomime of street actors and painters. Without much difficulty, she found the same streets and shops and for a few days already she was repeating her outings. With nice warm weather and the clear sky, she simply enjoyed walking the streets and looking at shop windows, almost forgetting the purpose of her strolls. She crossed the street and looked at the shop window again. "The silhouette! the same silhouette! It's not a mistake, that's him." Judy froze for a moment not knowing what to do; she did not want to scare him off again, and after a short meditation, she decided, "Well, what's the heck," and she turned around. This time, a young handsome fellow with a beret on the top of his brown, slightly reddish curly hair did not turn away, but instead slowly approached her.

"Who are you, and why are you following me?" Judy asked him

"My name is Etienne. We have to talk."

"Okay," Judy replied.

"We can go to a café," politely offered Etienne."

"Sure," she agreed.

They went to a café and took a table that was offered to them by a waiter. "Etienne, by the way, you awfully resemble your sister," remarked the waiter. Etienne pulled down his beret and they looked at each other noticing with much surprise that they both had brown slightly reddish waved hair, some barely perceptible similarity in their face traits, and an unmistakable dimple on their chins.

"Well," Judy mused "it probably happens, but not too often," not paying much attention to the waiter's remark.

Etienne ordered some beer, and she got herself soda with ice.

"I know who you are," said Etienne. "I saw you on TV."

"Of course," it struck Judy. During the conference there was the TV interview with Dr. van Bright, where Judy was also present along with other colleagues. She wore her medallion, which she practically never parted with.

"It was me at Notre Dame, dressed as a monk," he said. Judy suppressed her surging excitement. She did not know, was it good news or the bad, and does she have to be happy about it or quite on the contrary?

"Someone tried to tear off the medallion from my neck," started Judy and looked in his eyes.

"I know, I saw it, but I had nothing to do with it."

"Where did you get your medallion, Etienne?" asked Judy.

Etienne got his medallion from his grandfather, and the later got it as a gift when he came to age from one of the Jesuit monks. His grandfather was an orphan and grew up in a monastery. Etienne, himself, and his father, not being jewelers, have a passionate hobby of making jewelry. They both understood very well that part of the medallion is missing and for many years they tried to find its missing part and determine the origin of the unusual medallion. They had looked through multiple jewelry catalogs for many years, but all their efforts were completely unsuccessful.

Now, Judy could understand his interest in her medallion and why he showed her his part of the medallion in Notre Dame.

Etienne made a good impression on her and his story seemed to be truthful. When he offered for her to meet his parents who just arrived in Paris from their vacation in the countryside she readily agreed.

Judy arrived at a two-story house right on time and rang the bell. The door opened and she found herself in a spacious hall with a marble staircase, mirrors, and flowers. She went up to the second floor and was met by Nicolette, a pleasant and neatly dressed woman of approximately 50 years who led her to a drawing room where Monsieur Paul and Madame Vivien were already sitting and waiting for her.

Etienne belonged to the family of a French businessman. He himself was a talented musician and played the violin beautifully. They even tried to play together, and it came out very nice. Over dinner, Judy told her part of the story, and after the dinner Etienne removed his part of the medallion and asked Judy to do the same. He inspected both parts of the medallion very intently with a magnifying glass and other tools. Both parts were very similar, but not identical, especially the chain whose unique pattern and design was not possible to repeat. It looked like whoever created this medallion thoroughly thought it over. Nevertheless, two parts of the medallion including the chains complemented each other perfectly. Etienne carefully tried to assemble them and he succeeded. A marvelous transformation happened right under their eyes. The medallion changed its color, and instead of blood drops, a soft pink glow appeared. Marveling at the medallion for a little while, he tried to open it. The medallion opened up easily and a tiny, shiny object rolled out of it. Surprised, he started inspecting it under the magnifying glass. Judy believed that she knew what it was; the tiny angel shepherd boy on her icon was missing his pipe, and she thought it could be it.

It was so amazing that complete strangers living in different counties, different continents, whose ways had never crossed before, were united, nevertheless, by some common mystery. They all were very impressed and shaken, and nobody had a clue how it could possibly happen. Etienne put the object back and closed the medallion. After that, he disassembled it and returned Judy her part.

Etienne proposed some ideas. He offered Judy to visit a place, where he as a child had been taken several times by his grandfather and where they could try to find some clues to their puzzles. Judy agreed, and Etienne saw Judy to her hotel. The next morning, they met and together set off to the countryside.

17 THE MYSTERIOUS DOOR

Judy was marveling at the beautiful panorama of Paris and the suburbs opening before them while driving to their destination. Etienne briefed her about historical monuments and parks they encountered on their way, and perhaps because of it, their drive did not seem to be long. Soon, the white Peugeot drove up to the fence of an ancient church. Next to the church was a neatly kept graveyard. Armed with flashlights, ropes, helmets, and other useful things they got out of the car and headed toward one of the ancient vaults. Etienne opened a massive carved metal door with the key and they approached the tombstone. He easily moved it to the side and under it opened a spiral stone staircase. Etienne went down the stairs first lighting his way with the flashlight. Before them opened a green corridor. Etienne confidently was leading the way, and Judy followed him cautiously surveying the walls of the corridor, on which there were painted trees with green leaves, that created an impression of an alley. Between the trees, there were painted columns with lit lanterns on them. Etienne's confidence, however, soon passed to her. They walked for a little while and a wall ahead bared their way. To the right of the wall there was another staircase, which was not immediately noticeable. They went further underground, walking forward and passing corridor after corridor, passage after passage. Finally, they found themselves in an underground hall. Suddenly Etienne came to a halt and started to listen attentively.

"What is it?" asked Judy anxiously, straining her ears. It sounded as though a man and a woman, breathing heavily with tense efforts were trying their best.

"Lie still, Suzi. We cannot make it." The sounds were coming from some little distance away.

"Napoleon, laying still, is that our only choice now?"

"Yes, Suzi, I am afraid so."

"Suzi, Napoleon!?" exclaimed Judy completely bewildered, and almost out of breath.

"Is that you?" For a moment everything went silent.

"Doctor Green, we are caved in by eboulement and cannot get out."

"What are you doing here in the first place!?" exclaimed Judy. She did not get a reply; they went silent. Meantime Etienne, fully realizing the situation, was losing no time. He started examining the hall, trying to find out where exactly the voices were coming from. At last, an idea struck him and he approached two big boulders and tried to move aside one of them. A small hole opened behind it. He shone his flashlight in it and immediately the cheerful voices of Suzi and Napoleon were heard. But the cheers were still quite premature. Because of Suzi's plump and very round forms, getting her out of her entrapment was not an easy task at all. Nevertheless, with much effort Suzi and Napoleon both were finally extracted with, fortunately, only minor damages, just a few scratches.

There was no time for explanations, and the four of them continued their way in the underground labyrinths together. Suzi folded her walker because she did not really need it to walk. She actually used it to stack on it her trophies -- multiple magazines, books and her purse. One has to notice that she had a very special interest and attraction to all kinds of rustling papers, lovingly stacking them on the walker and in her purse.

They passed passage after passage, and it seemed as there would be no end of it.

"It's here! suddenly proclaimed Etienne," pointing to the passage that was barred by the wall ahead. They lit the corridor with their flashlights. At first sight, it was no different from many others, they had already passed. Judy approached the wall that barred the passage and started inspecting it with much curiosity and attention. The wall was faced with the small grey stones, surprisingly precisely selected by size and color, and were put together very neatly. It undoubtedly was the creation of highly skillful human hands.

"Exquisite workmanship," Judy mused, stroking the wall with the palm of her hand.

"What is it behind it? Does it hide the solution of our mystery, or does it open a new one?"

There was a stone bench by the wall also faced by small grey stones. Etienne and his grandfather would seat and rest on it after long passages through the endless corridors. Judy started inspecting thoroughly the small stones one by one trying to find some flaw but without avail. She couldn't find anything unusual in the wall.

Well, it looked like the corridor turned out to be simply another dead end, one of the many they encountered on their way. Judy had already decided that there was no use to stay here longer and it was time to go back. But instead, she suddenly and quite surprisingly for herself, turned around and went to another passage that also was barred by the wall faced with the small grey stones. The only difference between these two similar passages was a niche in the second passage located close to the ceiling in which one could see two human scalps and bones. She set to work again inspecting the wall carefully and attentively, and not finding anything peculiar again wearily leaned against it. She immediately felt a light sway, thinking she probably was getting dizzy underground. In an instant, however, she turned around and pushed the wall with all her strength. The wall moved slowly revealing behind it a heavy forged door. Now Judy knew exactly what she was going to do. Before the surprised eyes of her companions, she opened her backpack and pulled out of it her big carved key with tiny human scalps and bones, the one she retrieved from the secret compartment of her ancient trunk and with which she never parted, the one she called symbolically "My key to solution and the talisman." At that time, of course, she did not have an idea that the key would serve its direct purpose and is destined to open a mysterious door. The carved key seemed to fit the door slit perfectly and surprisingly turned without much effort. Judy pushed the heavy forged door and it opened. They all found themselves on the threshold of a spacious room that resembled a cave. Everybody was overcome with an understandable excitement. This door could lead them to the solution of their mystery, a mystery that was so thoroughly hidden from everybody for generations.

Lighting her way with a flashlight, Judy first crossed the threshold and entered the room. Everybody followed her.

18 IN THE CAVE

Entering the cave, they looked around and immediately noticed a massive roughly built table and some likeness of chairs around it. On the table there were scattered old papers and newspapers.

On the other side of the cave there was a deep ditch. It looked like some time ago a part of the cave had collapsed. Everybody immediately got busy looking around and inspecting the cave, and at first nobody noticed that in the semi darkness of the cave someone else had appeared. Suddenly, Judy again was overcome with some unexplainable, disquieting feeling, one that she had experienced before and she stopped and turned her head. Not far from her, Ray was standing. In spite that recently Judy had become used to many unexpected surprises and even shocks, she, nevertheless, was struck dumb. Recovering, she first of all tried to compose herself, and then cast a glance at him, inspecting him from his head to toes. He was dressed in an impeccable suit, a shirt with necktie, shoes, presumably with a squeak, and had a smile on his face. All his appearance was in complete discordance with the setting. Judy approached him with an unconcerned air. He was still smiling, slightly rubbing his forehead; to be more precise, he seemed to be hiding his eyebrow behind his hand, trying probably to remind her of a scene from her recent humorous novella.

"Well," she mused for a second, blowing off a lock of hair out of her forehead,

"I play by the rules," and she somehow put together all her strength, energy, and skills in one fist and with the lighting speed she delivered a sudden, precise, and crushing blow to his chin. Mr. Stranger, Steven McRae, Dracula, or simply Ray, as everybody called him at the hospital, rocked slightly and came crashing down. Everybody including Judy became rooted to the spot out of suddenness.

"Perfect knockout, Judy," she heard "Where did you learn it?"
Judy herself could not expect something like this to ever happen to her, and of course she could not explain how she actually delivered such a strong and precise blow. She stepped up to Ray, bent over him and "sisterly" checked his pulse.

"Well, it looks like we already exchanged our 'pleasantries,' and a 'warm-up' took place."

After that, Judy went to the table and began looking through the papers: the old newspapers, some drawings. It seemed to her that it was simply a waste of time to read them all. Inspecting the papers Judy mused, "two similar, but not identical medallions; two similar passages, but only one cave? Is it possible that there is somewhere another cave, and if so how to find it?"

Subconsciously, she started putting separately newspapers where the Russian name Orlofsky was mentioned, a fact that did not escape her attention. Now newspaper after newspaper, she started reading headlines: "Disappearance of Duke Orlofsky," "Duke Orlofsky and his Unique Jewelry Collection," "Search for the Famous Collection," "Soviet Government got on track of the Northern Lights" ....

Meanwhile, Suzi got to the table and was watching the rustling papers as charmed and with much admiration. It has to be said that she had an insurmountable desire to get them all in her possession and neatly stack them on her walker.

"The Northern Lights," Judy had heard of it; she had read about it somewhere. She had read about Duke Orlofsky and his famous jewelry collection by the name "Northern Lights." In the pre-revolutionary Russia, young Duke Orlofsky himself was an avid jeweler. He assembled a team of the best native talents-- jewelry makers to create a unique jewelry collection. From time to time, they would present their creations on the International Exhibitions and auctions and sell them for some large sums of money. The most famous and precious item in the collection was the

71

diadem "Northern Lights," that gave name to the entire collection. The diadem was made of precious metals-- gold, platinum, and silver and comprised a thousand diamonds and precious stones, meticulously selected by size, color and hue. Together they spread soft glow reminiscent of the Northern Lights. The diadem also contained the "Polar Star," one of the purest and largest diamonds in the world resembling a star by shape and that's why it got its name.

After the revolution and during the Soviet time, the Russian government conducted a persistent search for the collection, perseveringly trying to find it and return it to Russia. All their efforts, nevertheless, were completely futile and unsuccessful, for the Duke himself and his collection disappeared after the revolution without a trace.

Etienne meanwhile, was intently reading the newspapers that Judy put aside for him. Besides the newspapers, there were numerous drawings that Judy was looking through. On one of the drawings, she saw a medallion that looked similar to their medallion. She couldn't believe her eyes and handed the drawing to Etienne. He immediately took off his medallion and offered Judy to do the same. After that he carefully assembled the medallion and compared it with the drawing. The resemblance was simply stunning. The revelation shook them both to the core. Judy could not utter a ward, feelings overflowed her. She could not possibly imagine that her medallion and the family mystery behind it could have any even remote relation to Duke Orlofsky and his famous disappeared collection.

"Medallion," an unpleasant crisp voice suddenly was heard. Behind them, by the table, was standing an unknown man with a revolver and extended palm of his hand. At the entrance of the cave there was another one with a revolver -- Two unknown men with revolvers, whose appearance in the cave nobody had noticed. Judy hesitated, but she didn't have much choice and handed her medallion to the unknown man. He immediately put it in his pocket and began grabbing all the newspapers and drawings. Suzi, sitting on her walker nearby, grew snow white pale and seemed to be outraged. Right in front of her eyes someone was grabbing all these papers – a treasure, she fancied to possess herself.

"Oh, dear, dear, why such a rudeness," Judy heard Azelia's voice, and at that point she was not surprised at anything anymore.

"You see, my dearest, dearest late mother taught us good manners. And you know there were eight of as and all girls," went on gabbling Azelia.

"Can you imagine she called all her eight daughters Azaleas: Azalea Albus, Azalea, Pincus, Azalea Flavus, Azalea…" and she was counting fingers on her palm one by one. At this moment Jannete's shrill pierced the cave.

"I am so sick, so sick, so, so sick!" she howled trying to outshout Azelia.

"Shut up!" frantically cried the man with a gun, trying to cover his ears with his hands. At that very moment, one more amazing transformation happened. Unexpectedly to everyone present in the cave, Azelia delivered a strong blow with her high heel to the man's jaw and knocked out his weapon. In an instant, Azelia took off her shoes, a wig fell off her head and she immediately transformed to a man with strong muscles and fists. Meantime Ray, who was completely forgotten, came to and joined the fierce fight. Ultimately the robbers overpowered and got hold of their weapons. They grabbed all the papers and retired to the door. No sooner they had disappeared behind the door then sand and stones began falling intensely from the ceiling locking them up in the cave for the fierce fight and shaking of the cave did not pass without harm.

In the twinkling of an eye, the door was completely covered with sand and stones, so retreat was impossible and on the opposite side of the door there was only a deep ditch. With much regret and disappointment, they now found themselves walled up in the cave.

19 THE WELL

With every passing minute, the situation was becoming more and more alarming and dangerous. They had to act quickly and without delay, otherwise they all would be buried in sand and stones in no time.

Ray and Etienne tied a rope to one of the massive table legs, which by that time was almost completely covered with sand. Etienne walked up to the edge of the precipice and holding the rope, began descending. Ray was securing the rope. Tense minutes that felt like eternity, passed and everybody heard Etienne's voice.

"Over here, everybody over here. There is a staircase hitherward!"

It was, of course, unknown where this staircase could lead them and for how long their flashlight batteries would last, but there was no other choice and they agreed to go along with Etienne.

It turned out that below the cave in the precipice wall was a deep niche with a small landing in it which could not be seen from above. Out of that landing a staircase was leading further underground.

There was no time to lose. They decided to lower Suzi and Jannette first, then Judy, and after her, everybody else would follow. Suzi was tied with the rope and slowly lowered into the ditch. With Etienne's help, she safely reached the landing. The same way, one by one, they all descended into the ditch with Ray rearing the group. At last, everyone was there and fortunately without any serious injuries or accidents and with only a few scratches and some bruises because of the stones fallen that had them.

From one side of the staircase, there was a wall, and from the other – a deep ditch. Carefully, trying to keep closer to the wall, they started descending step by step to complete uncertainty deeper underground, and after a while the stairs became a little wider and they encountered a side passage. They followed into this narrow winding passage which led them to other passages, corridors, and staircases. The danger of the rockfall, cave-in, and the underground waters was there at all times, but they bravely moved forward without fear, tiredness, and almost without rest hoping that ultimately, they would find their way to the surface.

It was simply amazing that Suzi and Jannette bore with fortitude their underground tribulations, not mentioning the other members of the group. At last, the corridor they walked on started narrowing steadily, and the contours of the wall that would bar their moving onward appeared ahead.

Would their worst fears come true, and they, after all, came to another dead end? This alarming question, of course, was on everybody's mind because after all they went through there was no way of going back.

They accelerated their pace and now almost ran toward the wall. And, yes, it was the wall and it looked as nothing else was near or behind it. Nevertheless, they looked anxiously round and found out that the wall and a slight widening of the corridor right in front of the wall was encased with wooden logs. They tried to inspect the ceiling then with their flashlights much-dimed by that time. Lights wouldn't reach the ceiling, but simply dissolved in the darkness.

"What is it, some kind of a well or what?"

Ray and Etienne immediately started climbing up wooden logs. Etienne went first and after a while one of the logs under Etienne's leg crushed down and he hung dangerously by his hands. Ray was in time to put his shoulder under his leg. Helping each other, they soon reached the top which was covered with a wooden lid. They knocked out the lid and got out, finding themselves in an abandoned coal mine. It was an old and deep coal mine but, nevertheless, they found their way out and got to the surface. Walking out of the mine they found themselves in the thick woods. A clear starry sky without a single cloud and high trees were all around them. A forest meadow flooded with moonlight could also be seen not far away.

In less than a half an hour, a helicopter was circling the meadow. Upon landing, the rescue group extracted everybody from the well. Then retrieved Suzi's walker, which she loved so much that she would not abandon it while passing through the endless underground passages.

Excited exclamations, embraces, and simply gladness filled the air. They were safe!

After all the strain and excitement, they had to embrace during their underground trip, it felt so amazing to be on the surface again and inhale with their whole chests, the invigorating freshness of evening cool.

But what is it on Suzi's walker, dazzlingly shining and gleaming under the light projectors?

Not believing their eyes, everybody exclaimed

"Medallion!!!"

Unbelievable, Judy was ready to sit on the ground and cry with excitement. It was their medallion, but how?

In the most critical moment when the gun was pointed at them, virtuoso Suzi brilliantly managed to steal the medallion from the robber when he was grabbing her precious rustling papers from the table.

Well, it's Suzi!

At that very moment, Judy was fairly happy that treatment of her patient had apparently failed, but she also assumed that the extreme situation they had found themselves underground, could trigger her kleptomaniac patient to relapse.

When all the excitement and embraces subsided, Judy cast an inquiring glance at everyone, and her inquiry was understood without a single word.

"How had they all happened to get into Paris catacombs?"

A short silence followed and Jannette brought herself to answer for everybody.

"Doctor Green, we were worrying about you and agreed that you shouldn't take such a dangerous trip alone." The answer, of course, was quite "exhaustive." However, her question was also related to Ray and she turned her gaze at him. Their eyes met. In response, he evasively rubbed his jaw with his hand and the corners of his eyes gleamed that barely perceptible ironic smile.

Later on, Judy pondered many times over that knockout. How she could possibly deliver such a strong and precise blow, after all, she had never taken up boxing.

In spite of the seeming cruelty of this sport, Judy loved boxing especially the techniques of the grand champions. As Judy has always liked some philosophical reflections, in her heart she would draw a parallel between boxing and the real life.

"Circumstances and turns of fate could be cruel and unexpected and could hit you just as well as fists do. Hence, be prepared for them, do not miss blows, and be ready to shield and defend yourself."

The helicopter brought the travelers to Paris, where a French emergency unit took care of their scratches and bruises. They all refused hospitalization because they were feeling fine. Besides, because of the overflowing gladness, they even forgot about their tiredness.

Judy invited Etienne to visit her in Los Angeles and meet her grandmother in Florida. Suzi returned the medallion to Judy and they split it with Etienne restoring its previous shape. Soon, Judy and company left Paris and returned home to Los Angeles.

Judy's trip to Paris was meant to bring some clarifications to the recent happenings around her and to untangle the tangled ball, but it seemed that the ball was getting more and more entangled and the unraveling of the mystery moves further and further away. It seemed as she would need considerable efforts to get a good understanding of the unusual happenings and solve the mystery of the ancient medallion and the trunk.

Part Two

20 THE PREMONITION

****

Russia, Arkhangelsk Province. Beginning of 20th Century

A noonday swelter is unbearable. A wayfarer suffering from scorching heat, thirst, and tiredness pauses to look around. Blood is throbbing in his temples and his head is ready to split in half from debilitating pain. An endless steppe lies before him, stretching in all directions as far as he can see. But he is exhausted and has no strength to move forward.

A black raven spreading wide its wings soars over his head in the clear blue sky without a single cloud as if trying to shield him from that red-hot fiery ball so relentlessly searing him with its blistering rays. Insistently and relentlessly, the raven follows the wayfarer, circling over him, descending lower and lower. Unable to move a single muscle anymore, the wayfarer falls to the ground.

"Water, water, water, a sip of water, please," he mumbles helplessly. Meanwhile, the wing beats come closer and closer and he can almost feel them with his skin.

Suddenly, cool, fresh, and moist air begins to blow softly out of no-where, and a splash of reviving water could be heard.

"Water! Could it possibly be water nearby?" flashed in his inflamed brain, and gathering his all might and strength, he tries to get back on his feet to reach it. But no, an incredible force pushes him back to the ground making his body very heavy and unable to move. His eyelids close and a spectacular scenery and a picturesque view emerges in his imagination

Glittering under the bright summer sun, a calm azure blue sea just slightly ruffling its surface was soothingly bathing the sandy beaded shore. A white ship like a sea gull approaching the shore was sliding over the surface, barely touching the water. There were the nearest and dearest people to his heart on that ship, gaily and nonchalantly indulging themselves in enjoyment and delight.

But what is it? Suddenly the sky overcast and the strong wind starts to blow. With the increasing wind blasts, the sea rises, and the terrible storm breaks out. The squall gusts whirl up mighty waves that pounce upon the ship and she starts to lurch and submerge deeper into the water. The caressing azure sea vanishes and the dark bubbling waves start to change their color under the raging thunder and lightnings thrown out by the heavens. On the top of the brutal waves that have acquired a bloody red color, an enormous number of fish appear.

"But wait," the wayfarer looks harder, "are they fish or the fish heads?" Unwittingly he asks himself a question. Immediately his entire body shudders from terrible fright when he realizes that these are neither fish, nor fish heads; these are human scalps, an immense quantity of them!

Huge waves continue to overflow the ship, and disaster seems inevitable. They all will perish in this bloody whirlpool! The wayfarer strains himself in one last attempt to stand up and rush to rescue. But all in vain. The same force and heaviness push him back to the ground and he cannot move.

"Raven, black raven, you left me, where have you gone?" He mumbled in despair. But there was no black raven anymore. Instead, a white, blue-eyed angel with dark, almost black beautiful hair, leaned over him beating its wings worryingly and emanating cool freshness, and tender care.

The patient was tossing and turning in delirium in bed. He was very sick and had a high fever.

"Water, water, water, a sip of water, please," he begged continuously in a feeble voice, barely moving his dried lips. Suddenly, he raised his heavy eyelids and opened his eyes. He couldn't recognize the ambience, neither could he recognize those people with kind faces bustling around him. Everything was completely unknown. A blue-eyed angel at his bed-head leaned over him and put caringly on his forehead something white and cool. One more time he tries to free himself from the restraining hands and get up, however, his effort is powerless. He failed, and had to lay back to his pillows.

It had been already several days and nights that the household of Alexander Varnavich Rechachev ran off their feet taking turns and watching the patient at his bedside without closing their eyes. The patient's condition was very serious and in spite of all the energetic measures that had been undertaken, his high fever would not remit. He remained delirious and agitated, constantly trying to get out of bed.

A "Young Noblemen," as he has been christened by the villagers, was dug out from the snow pile on Christmas day, and brought to the Alexander Varnavich house barely alive. The ten-year-old daughter of Alexander Varnavich, Elizaveta, during the morning ride on her favorite, raven-black horse in a snow-covered field had spotted a huge, strange, snow pile that looked like an overturned sleigh. The preceding Christmas night was especially cold and snowy one. On seeing the snow pile and horses nearby, the quick-witted girl immediately realized that some travelers could lose their way during the raging severe snowstorm, wandered out of the high road, and had their sleigh overturned. Without losing time, she put her horse into a gallop and rushed back to the village.
It was early Christmas morning. The lively girl, who was very well known and respected among the villages for her deftness, came galloping to the village, and made there quite a commotion. She shook the entire village out of sleep, pulled sleepy villagers from their cozy beds and gathered folks with buckboards. Together they reached the snow pile. They dug up the overturned sleigh and pulled out of it a nobleman and a coachman, commonly called in Russia, a yamschik. Neither of the men showed any

thread of life, nevertheless, villagers brought them both to the village eying them with curiosity, and expressing their compassion.

"Oh, what a misfortune, what a misfortune befell them,"

"Look, the nobleman seems to be an important one," meaningfully remarked one of the villagers.

"Hey, Paltiucha, get me that mirror, will you?" commanded Nikitich in whose house they all had gathered. Paltiucha scratched his nape wondering "Why a mirror?" but brought the mirror obediently anyway. Nikitich took the mirror from Paltiucha and with the air of an expert, immediately placed it close to the sufferer's lips and nose by turns and everybody fell still in anticipation of what would happen next. The mirror slightly fogged.

"Breathing, breathing, he is alive!" resounded immediately.

"The nobleman is alive!" shouted the villagers in animation. And it did not take them long to decide what to do next. They all agreed on taking the barely alive nobleman to the house of a healer reputable in the whole county, Alexander Varnavich, and that is what they did without a delay. The unfortunate yamschik, frozen to death, was buried in the churchyard with the ringing of bells.

Alexander Varnavich sank wearily into his comfortable armchair in the library, where he loved to spend long winter evenings bending over his books. Sad thoughts tormented him. In spite of all the energetic efforts undertaken by his family, including numerous consultations with the Doctor, the patient's condition remained very serious and there were no signs of improvement. The patient continued to be feverish, delirious, and agitated. Nevertheless, Alexander Varnavich had full confidence in the efficacy of his wholesome herb treatment, that he had practiced for many years, and besides, deep inside in his heart, he sincerely believed that this young and strong body would get over the ailment and recover.

Stately, blue eyed, with noble face features and light brown hair, Newcomer, how Alexander Varnavich called him, immediately evoked good feelings in his household and among villagers alike.

"Nonetheless, who is he, and what stroke of fate has brought him to this part of the world?"

At this moment his thread of thoughts was interrupted by a tap on the door and with soundless footsteps, Anna one of his daughters, flit into the library.

"Father, father," barely repressing overflowing her excitement she uttered.

"The patient is all in sweat; it looks like his fever is falling."

She pushed back her dark, almost black curls, uncovering a dazzling white, slightly pinkish complexion. On her plush pink lips sparkled up a contemplative smile and her expressive blue eyes were glowing with childlike gladness.

The patient started sweating profusely; his fever had remitted, and it seemed like the crisis had passed. They immediately changed his sweaty sheets and clothes and put him in a dry, clean, and warm bed. After that moment, the patient's condition started improving steadily. Undoubtedly, besides all the curative measures undertaken, beneficial effects on his health were exerted by the wonderful qualities of fresh northern fish like beluga, starry sturgeon, summer salmon, humpback salmon, and black and red caviar that were supplied to the household on a regular basis in large quantities, and thanks to which, to a great extent Alexander Varnavich's commerce and business was blooming. Besides, sweet-smelling northern berries, mushrooms, and freshly drawn milk, and especially prolonged horse-back ridings in a fresh air saturated with pine, also contributed to his miraculous recovery.

All good-natured households of Rechachev sincerely got attached to Newcomer, and every one of them did their best to contribute and speed up his recovery. The Newcomer took special pleasure in horse-back riding with Anna and Elizaveta. All three of them were excellent riders and shared genuine love to these noble animals. This love brought them closer together and initiated their friendship.

Nevertheless, unanswered questions remained.

"Who is he, and what brought him to this part of northern Russia in the midst of a severe snowstorm?" Nobody could give answers, not even the Newcomer himself. In spite of recovering his physical strength, the severe overcooling his body was exposed to had exerted serious consequences to his health. He lost his long-term memory and because of that, everything preceding the accident was completely erased.

Meanwhile, Alexander Varnavich, convinced that immediate danger to the health of the patient has passed, went on to take his business trip and attend urgent governmental and commercial affairs leaving the recovering patient to the care of his folks.

The house was silent, all daily bustle and turmoil had calmed down and only the grandfather's clock beating time was heard. Praskoviya Artemievna couldn't get to sleep as something was bothering her, and she got up and threw on her shoulders a warm woolen shawl. She took a walk around the house and peeped into the children's bedrooms. They were sleeping peacefully, slightly snuffling their noses. She approached one of the windows that faced the road, and drew back the heavy curtain. High starry heavens and the tops of dark fir-trees like fairy-tale giants came into view under the softly falling moonlight. Something made her cast a glance at the looming dark woods in the distance, the winter road, and snow-covered fields. Suddenly, she noticed some movement on the road and she looked harder. Two dark, barely discernible human figures, came off the road and set off toward the house. She was immediately overcome with troubled thoughts.

"Who are they, what are they doing there on the road in the middle of the night?"

Meantime, the dark figures came closer to the house, paused in front of it, and observed it attentively. It seemed that they were exchanging some remarks. Fear fettered her entire body and she watched them, holding her breath. Finally, they turned around and moved away. She stood for a while by the window and after ascertaining herself that they were gone, returned to her bedroom but, of course, for long while couldn't fall asleep.

Meanwhile, in St. Petersburg, Duke and Duchess Orlofsky were deeply worried and concerned about the sudden disappearance of their only son, young Duke Peter Orlofsky. Being an enthusiastic jeweler and a collector of the precious gem stones, young Duke departed incognito to Archangelsk province, where rare Russian precious and semiprecious stones were found.

The disappearance of young Duke Orlofsky was broadly discussed in high society saloons and chambers and whereby the most varied speculations and conjectures were expressed. Private detectives hired by his parents by no means could get on his track and several months passed before some piece of information of his possible whereabouts and a feeble hope for his return appeared.

Meantime, Alexander Varnavich, after settling all his urgent business matters and affairs, returned home. The investigation he conducted himself and the data obtained suggested that young nobleman was none other than young Duke Orlofsky, a person close to the Sovereign. His assumptions were confirmed when private detectives came to the house and tried to explain to the Duke his identity and ancestry. However, no matter how hard they tried, all their efforts were of no avail. The young Duke was completely unable to recollect anything from his previous life but, nevertheless, he conceded to their insistent persuasions and returned to Petersburg making his parents and relatives happy beside themselves.

In order to recover his memory, he underwent multiple consultations with doctors and treatment abroad. All the energetic curative measures conducted finally took effect, and he gradually started to regain his memory.

Young Duke Orlofsky again found himself engrossed in concerts, receptions, and suppers and surrounded by military officers, red-cheeked hussars, and ladies, dressed according to the latest Paris fashion and with sparkling jewelry. Nevertheless, a blue-eyed angel with dazzling white skin and dark curly hair with whom he associated his rescue, recovery, and return to his customary life and environment was emerging in his imagination more and more often. She followed him insistently and relentlessly and thoughts of her filled his heart with unexplainable tenderness and warmth. The attempts to out-dazzle the radiance of those beautiful, kind, and caring eyes, to forget their cheerful riding in the woods, and his timid courtship, that she was accepting favorably, were not crowned with success.

Several months passed and the decision to return to Alexander Varnavich's family and ask for the hand of his daughter, Anna, was coming to his heart. The Duke was well aware, that by marrying a charming being of lower ancestry, he would bring upon himself the outrage of respected people dearly loved by him, and it was quite possible that neither his parents, nor the Sovereign would ever give their consent to his marriage. Nevertheless, he made his firm and steadfast decision.

21 JUDY RETURNS FROM PARIS

On return from Paris, Judy and company's life began to follow its customary stream way. Judy's patients and research work awaited her, and
she actively got back to business. The Inseparable Four plus Jannette,
united as ever before as a team, underwent "baptism by fire," and so effi-
ciently supported Judy at the right time and right place, went back to their
usual pastime and it looked like the excitements experienced in Paris
drew them even closer together. Nonetheless, more and more often they
isolated themselves from others showing some signs of secretiveness.
Judy continued her insistent attempts to find out how on earth they all
came to appear in the Paris catacombs at such a crucial moment for her
stroke against the insurmountable barrier. They would immediately with-
draw into themselves and no information could she possibly pry out of
them. However, thanks to Suzi's extraordinary "talent," the medallion
was saved and returned to Judy and for that she was deeply grateful to
her. The revelation of a possible connection between her medallion,
Etienne, and Duke Orlofsky and his famous and richest jewelry collection
became for Judy a stunning discovery, but at the same time, significantly
complicated her tasks. The exciting questions "How, when, and on what
turn of fate they all have been inter-twisted?" emerged in her mind more
and more often, as she realized, that there will be no easy way to find it
all out. She knew, that searching for the Duke and his collection was conducted unsuccessfully by the former soviet government for many years,
and that her attempts to unravel a family mystery may intersect with their

search, and, as she already found out in Paris, it was fraught with danger. Nevertheless, to stop at half-way was not in her character and she firmly resolved to continue her adventure. For this purpose, she needed to contemplate a plan for her further actions and coordinate it with Etienne. The trip to Paris that she undertook to clarify the matter, in reality, raised in front of her new questions: who tried to tear off the medallion from her neck, who prevented the theft, and who were those people that attacked them in the catacombs? Besides, who had ransacked her house and why, what they were looking for? The most important question, however, was whether all these happening were somehow linked with each other or not. The search in her house happened right after their visit to Our Bear Garden city. What if there was another reason for that, a reason, she cannot even think about now. How confident is she in her patients, with whom she has longstanding and slightly exceeding conventional Doctor-patient interrelationships? And also, how confident is she in the efficacy of her treatment and their recovery, and could it be that their criminal past had something to do with it? Judy was asking herself all these questions many times as she was trying to sort everything out.

Judy, together with Doctor Van Bright completed their morning patient round and were satisfied with the results of their treatment. Nevertheless, she had some concerns about one of new patients of hers that she intended to discuss with Doctor Van Bright. Young veteran experienced perseverant and excessive combat recollections. With unfading clarity, they emerged in his mind making him go through psychologically traumatic events over and over again. His condition hasn't improved in the span of several years and deeply reflected on his family and those around him. Being unable to extinguish his emotional stress and, related to it aggressive outbursts, he resorted to alcohol and drugs.

Judy set forth to doctor Van Bright the patient' condition and her plans for treatment.

To ease his response to traumatic recollections, and ultimately extinguish the "flashpoint" of their origin on the first place, Judy wanted to help him understand the neurobiological nature of his malady, and instill in him an unshakeable hope and confidence in recovery. To carry out with her plan she was going to conduct combination therapy including psychotherapy and pharmacological treatment, that would allow her to repair the disturbed balance of important biologically active molecules in his central nervous system.

"Judy, I completely agree with your choice of drugs in combination with psychotherapy, and I also like your approach and aspiration to invigorate his will of power and his confidence in recovery. Yes, one more thing, I hope you will continue your consultations and psychotherapy over the internet after his discharge."

"Oh, sure, we will continue his treatment over internet, since access to high-skilled psychiatric care, at this point, is somehow restricted in the area of his residency."

"Very well, then. By the way, about your trip to Paris. Any news?" asked Doctor Van Bright.

Earlier on, Judy had related to him about meeting Etienne and his family, about her adventures and the danger they encountered in the catacombs. Doctor Van Bright had listened to her that time with big attention and sympathy, offering his help and support should she need it.

"Oh no, not yet. It's just that Etienne is coming to Florida to meet my grandma. Onward we will continue our investigation together."

"Well, good luck and keep me informed."

Judy left his office and went to conduct psychotherapy over the internet with another patient of hers. After that, she was ready for the flight to Florida to meet Etienne and grandma.

On completing her packing, she headed off to the airport and left for Jacksonville. She anxiously awaited meeting with Etienne. How quaint it is, by some inscrutable ways that they are connected through the mysterious medallion and concealed behind it a family secret.

"Will they succeed in their endeavor and unravel the mystery?" At this time, it was hard to say, but the firmness and willpower experienced by both of them in critical moments during their dangerous underground tour in Paris, give them both confidence and trust for each other.

"Hi, Etienne, welcome to Florida," Judy spotted him and waved at him at the baggage claim, when he arrived in Jacksonville

"Hi, Judy, how are you?"

They exchanged their greeting, received baggage, and headed to grandmother's. There she introduced Etienne to grandmother, and told her all about the trip to Paris, and about their findings, causing her great astonishment.

"Very interesting," slightly tilting her head sideways she said pensively, and in her still beautiful green eyes, flashed an ethereal mist.

"Nothing like this would ever cross my mind," she said.

Before commencing thorough examination of papers recovered from her great-grandmother's trunk, Judy intended to check out her supposition and give a try to a tiny object hidden in the medallion. In front of grandmother's amazed eyes, Etienne reunited two parts of the medallion and instead of the red "blood drops" a pink, soft radiance spread out. Etienne opened the medallion and a small shiny object popped out. He carefully tried to place it in the hands of a shepherd boy on the elaborately carved box with the icon. The object fitted perfectly by shape and size. Then he advanced it further and slightly pressed on it. Immediately, a lengthwise split appeared and the box could be opened easily. On opening the box, he carefully pulled out the icon. Behind the icon, to everybody's amazement, a beautiful painting was hidden. On the painting a spectacular scenery was portrayed - huge mountains with snow covered tops surrounded by green hills. A majestic cathedral of Byzantine style was towered on one of them as a quiescent and stern guardian, watchfully safeguarding all these fairy beauties. Right there at sight, a waterfall was taking its cold swift waters to a highland lake. In the right lower corner of the painting, there was something resembling a blueprint. A smooth wall showed a small niche in which the outline of an icon could be perceived. Under the blueprint, there was an inscription, presumably the author's signature. Judy, who could speak the Georgian language, brought a loupe and started examining the signature. It turned out to be the name of the region and of the cathedral in Republic of Georgia.

"Well, puzzle after puzzle," Judy said to herself.

"The more we uncover, the more complicated it gets!"

She was right, though. The tiny pipe, hidden in the medallion, really was a missing part of the box, allowing to open it.

Laying aside for a while the icon and the painting, they started examining the papers found in the secret compartment of the trunk. Yellowed pages, one by one, were looked through, read over, and neatly piled up. Regretfully, reading papers did not bring them any additional clues or clarifications. They turned out to be tender letters of two loving hearts separated and immensely longing for each other.

The painting of the cathedral with the name of the region, hidden along with the icon so elaborately, gave the idea that the cathedral somehow has something to do with their medallion and its mystery and, hence, Judy and Etienne had to visit it as soon as possible.

Judy returned to Los Angeles from Florida where she bade farewell to Etienne and her grandma. In the hospital, news awaited her. Rumor had it that the investigation was closed because the body was not found, and Hector turned out to be alive. Nonetheless, Doctor Van Bright insisted that the actor, or someone disguised as an actor, was dead, and that in front of the audience and troupe a crime was committed. Therefore, he contacted his cousin Doctor Mark Van Bright, who on multiple occasions rendered invaluable assistance to Police in solving crimes, and to his son, Steven, who no longer participated in investigations himself, but held high office in the Los Angeles Police.

It was hard to say whether the investigation was still ongoing or not, as officially it was closed, and all the activities in the club house were resumed. Little by little the incident started fading from everybody's memory.

The consequences of Steven's involvement, however, were not long in coming. Wasting little time, all the troupe was scrupulously traced, and it turned out, that one of the actors, a computer engineer, presumably vacationing in Bahamas, vanished. He simply didn't return from his vacation. All attempts to find him were not successful. An assumption was made that these two events could be connected to each other. Numerous viewing of the play tapes didn't elicit anything suspicious, but one couldn't rule out that the tapes were doctored. A concealed observation over play participants and club activities ensued. Did criminals buy that the investigation was over? They, however, knew very well that the Police had nothing to catch hold on at present time.

Grey mouse wheeled up to the club house and parked. Judy got out of the car and swiftly walked into the club. On entering the spacious and well-lit hall, she looked around. People were gradually filling it up and taking seats at the Bingo tables. Preparations for the game were in full swing. The inseparable Four plus Jannette proceeded to one of the secluded tables by the wall. Judy, surveying the hall several times, finally spotted them. Suzy, with her customarily rolled up sleeves, was busily laying on the table Bingo cards, now and then bringing her beautiful ring shaped as a big letter S with a sparkling stone, close to her lips. On noticing them, Judy immediately approached their table. At that moment Suzy shot a swift, lighting-like look at Napoleon.

"Hi, Judy, glad to see you. How are you doing, anything new?" Judy moved up to one of the empty near-by chairs and helped herself sit down by their table.

"All is well, thank you. It's been long time. I wanted to talk to you," she replied.

"How, how to do it, how to untie their tongues and get the information she needed?" floated in her mind, and offhandedly she decided to grab the bull by the horns, and get immediately down to business.

"My house had been ransacked," and significantly lowering her voice, she asked.

"Is there anything you would like to tell me? What was it all about?" At this moment Suzy and Napoleon exchanged swift glances. By their immediate reaction, Judy realized that she had stroked the right key and hit the target. They were concealing something important from her.

After a conversation with Gruben in Our Bear Garden, it became clear for Suzy, that the Farmers Bear statue comprised some value and was stolen for a reason. Rummage in their houses and apartments confirmed it, and, of course, put them on the alert. The theft, that took place during her staying there, a figure of significant authority-virtuoso in the thievish world of her past, could mean, that someone was trying to throw the shadow of suspicion at her and, hence, she could be caught in crisscross

92

fire. The situation was becoming serious and dangerous not only for her and her friends, but also for unsuspecting and completely unaware of anything, Judy. Some inquires, she had conducted so far, didn't bring her any significant clarifications, and she had nothing to say to Judy, not just yet.

"Doctor Green, we are truly glad to see you, and would like to have a frank talk with you, we promise, but at this time we have nothing to say." Now, Judy, at least, could assume that something happened during their stay in Our Bear Garden, something that her "squad" is hiding from her, and that the rummage in her house could be unrelated to her medallion. This significantly changes the matter.

"Disappearance of the statue! Who could possibly look for the stolen statue in my house? Well, if they could steal the statue of the Farmers bear, be sure, they could steal something else. They are quite experts at that." She chuckled to herself.

22 THE FURY AND EXPULSION

***

Russia, Arkhangelsk province
End of 1916 and beginning of 1917 year

On a frosty winter evening at the outskirts of the northern town, a nuptial sacrament was taking place. Numerous glimmering candles, being reflected from polished gilded icons, lighted up a chamber in a small church and a smell of burned incense could be sensed. Gilded wreathes were placed over the heads of the bride and groom and a chant of churchmen annunciated: "Servant of God, Anna, is joining in marriage Servant of God, Peter...."

Attendees were smitten by the good looks of the young couple, standing by the altar--a tall handsome man dressed in severe black attire and a bride in a white silk wedding gown. Her dark, almost black hair, flowed on her dazzling white marbled shoulders, her beautiful, expressive, blue eyes beamed with happiness that couldn't be outshone by the sparkling precious stones of her exquisite necklace and a marvelous medallion, presented to her by the Duke for the wedding.

Outside the church fence a harnessed sleigh was waiting for them. The trotters, impatiently stumping their hoofs against frozen ground, were snorting and tossing their manes as if anticipating a drastic change in weather. The heavens began to gloom gradually and gather gray snow clouds. The stars were now barely perceptible, and a bright, bathed, moon was playfully emerging and hiding behind clouds. Snow began. Falling white, lacy snowflakes, skillfully enweaved by some mysterious crafts-man, were immediately snatched up by the angry northern wind, spanned in the round dance, and dropped down to the ground, densely wrapping it up in white blanket.

Upon completion of the ceremony, the happy couple, bundled up in costly furs, was whisked into the night by a trio of horses with jingling bells. These were the young Duke and Duchess Orlofsky, heading to one of his estates, where he hoped to obtain from his parents and the Sover-eign forgiveness for his secret and unequal marriage and shortly return with his spouse to Petrograd.

However, their expectations fell short. Very soon it became clear that neither forgiveness nor blessings would be obtained. Furthermore, the fury exceeded all expectations and he was immediately exiled to the Cau-casus.

After Alexander Varnavich and Praskoviya Artemievna gave Anna in marriage, their daughter Maria and the younger children remained in the house. From the study, where Alexander Varnavich liked to seclude him-self, sounds of music could be heard as he was giving the violin lessons to his daughter Maria. Meanwhile a sleigh drove up to the house and the noise and shouts spread all over it – "Matchmakers, matchmakers, match-makers arrived."

Not a week passed since Anna was married, matchmakers came to Ma-ria, proposing her for husband a handsome, very skillful, and knowledge-able young man. His family, as he himself, had a very successful business that dominated the entire supply of hazel grouse to Petersburg. The matchmaker himself, once passionately enamored with Praskoviya Arte-mievna, a tall and beautiful lassie with blue eyes and a splendid blond plait, reputed as the first beauty in the county, was denied her hand. None-theless, his feelings for her were evidently still smoldering in his heart for quite some time, and when many years later he raised his only son, he resolved to marry him to her daughter, Maria.

The matchmaker reminded Alexander Varnavich events of long-gone days saying, "I was not destined to become the husband of Praskoviya

Artemievna, although I was dearly in love with her, so do not deny my son to marry her daughter, Maria."

Well, after such a disarming introduction, the matter was settled, and shortly Maria, too, got married.

During one of Alexander Varnavich business trips, when only the younger kids and Praskoviya Artemievna remained in the house an event with tragic consequences for the family had occurred. In the absence of her husband, Praskoviya Artemievna oftentimes would wake up in the middle of the night and for a long while couldn't go back to sleep. This time, too, she woke up, bundled up in a warm woolen shawl and stepped out of her bedroom. As usual, she went to the children's bedrooms to look at her peacefully sleeping kids. Some worrisome feelings came over her again and, leaving their bedrooms, she approached one of the windows, drew back heavy curtain, and looked out. A frosty night, the twinkling stars, and the bathed in moonlight field appeared to be the same, but wait, something is moving there again. She looked harder. Two dark figures moved away from the road and started approaching the house again.

"Is it real or, am I dreaming? If not, who are they and why they are coming close to the house so late at night?" It had happened before; she remembered it very well, and she had told her husband about that incident when he returned from his business trip.

In the meantime, dark figures approached the house again and started to look intently for something.

"What are they doing, what are they looking for?" hammered in her head and the chilling fear got hold of her entire body. She anxiously watched them out of the window. Finally, they found something and pulled it close to the window.

"A ladder, they are pulling a ladder to the window. These are robbers and they are trying to sneak into the house!" She has to act, and act very quickly or a disaster will inevitably happen!
Without losing a single minute, she rushed to the kitchen and grabbed the axe and ran back to the window. The robbers, meantime, already had gotten to the window-sill and were trying to open the window. In ferocious fury, she lifted the exe and shouted angrily at the top of her voice,

"Well, who has extra hands or head, get it in and I will chop it off at once!"

The robbers looked at her face distorted with anger and the lifted axe, looked at each other, and hastily backslide the ladder and disappeared. She stood for a while by the window, her warm shawl slipping off. She slowly went back to children's bedrooms where they were still sleeping. The danger has passed, and they all were saved. Experiencing the terrible excitement, though, had a deep detrimental effect on her health. Soon she fell seriously ill and passed away of a heart attack, leaving behind her kids and an inconsolable Alexander Varnavich.

Already pregnant, Anna returned home for her mother's funeral and decided to stay in the house until her childbirth and to take care of the younger kids and widowed and deeply mourning father, who did not live for long after his beloved wife's death.

Before departing for Caucasus, the Duke and Duchess split up the medallion. Half of it remained with Anna, and the other half she put around his neck. Thus, the heart was divided in two. They both sincerely believed and hoped, that time would settle down everything, that the fury would not last forever, and that sooner or later they would be forgiven, reunite, and live happily ever after.

However, their hopes and expectations were not meant to be realized, since in Russia a political situation was brewing up. The revolution and following the revolution Bolshevik take-over, Red terror, dictatorship, and civil war took tenths of millions of human lives, destroyed and scattered families around the world. As it turned out, the Duke's departure for Caucasus and later to Trans Caucasus and abroad right before the beginning of these events, saved his life.

After parting from the Duchess, the Duke uneventfully accomplished his passage from Russia to Caucasus and further to Trans Caucasus, to Georgia, where he visited the ancient city Tiflis. Founded in the fifth century, this city was conveniently situated on the banks of the river Mtkvari in a gorge that protected it from all winds. The special charm of this ancient city in which West meets East in its salient originality, colorfulness, and multinationalism mesmerized travelers. It was the city, where the houses with elaborately carved balconies, arranged and stacked one above the other on the hills, contrasted with the magnificent buildings of opera house, classical gymnasium, palace of vice-regent, and impressive cathedrals, and where narrow streets coexisted with broad avenues. How not to mention the famous Tiflis sulfur bath-houses, of which the great Russian poet Alexander Pushkin once wrote in his work "The Trip to Arzrum," that he had never seen in his entire life, not in Russia, not in Turkey anything so splendid as Tiflis bath-houses.

The complex harmony, distinctiveness, and beauty of Georgian folk songs and dances, that are an integral part of Georgian nation and traditions, along with Georgian hospitality, delicious food and vine, complemented the picture and created unforgettable and inerasable impressions. The Duke shared his enthusiastic feelings in his letters to his Duchess, who after delivery was contemplating joining him in Georgia. Unfortunately, ill fate befell on the young couple, still happy, in spite of all the happenings. Duchess Anna delivered twins: a boy and a girl and shortly succumbed to a difficult delivery. The outcast, grieving, and inconsolable Duke resolved to disengage from the worldly life and settled down in one of the high-mountain monasteries in Georgia.

Alarming news started reaching him up from Russia: the warfare, the revolution that finally was carried out, the Bolshevik take-over, and the sweeping of the entire country by brutal violence and bloodshed. These all compelled him to make a decision to abandon the Empire, go abroad, and take his children to safety.

23 SUZY CONDUCTS AN INVESTIGATION

Narrowing her naughty dark eyes with delight, Suzy took a sip from a cup of her favorite beverage-- hot chocolate with marshmallow, and put the cup carefully back on the saucer. She opened up her purse, and as was her custom, pulled out of it one of the numerous packs of cards. Suzy laid out the cards on the table with her plump hands, every now and then bringing her beautiful ring to her lips. Napoleon, who was sitting right across the table with a massive glass tabletop, also enjoyed the hot chocolate, dipping in it every once in a while, with a lemon-almond biscotti. He wouldn't take his eyes from her, watching her every move and trying to guess the train of her thoughts.

"Napoleon, just recently, Gruben's daughter, Jill Lee, appeared in the hospital. What do you think about it?" and not waiting for his reply stated,

"I believe, that Gruben himself is somewhere nearby, and that they are definitively up to something."
Her thoughts were intently working.

"Did Gruben have something to do with the theft of the paintings from the mega yacht, and why did the disappearance of the Farmer's Bear statue alarm him so strongly?" She needed to find everything out. What did she presently know?

"First of all, when the theft occurred, Gruben served as a security officer, but there was no incriminating evidence against him that time. Nevertheless, he was accused of negligence that entailed the theft.

Secondly, there was someone else connected to the investigation as a witness and, as she subsequently found out, it was Gruben's long-time friend, Jo Garner. They both served in the Police force and at one time were even partners in New Jersey. Were they involved in the theft? She also knew that Jo Garner was employed by the museum and sailed on the yacht during the exposition and theft.

Their visit to Our Bear Garden coincided with the festivities and celebrations of the 300th year anniversary of the city and also with a research conference conducted there annually. The city, hence, was flooded with tourists. Nevertheless, the coincidental presence there of Suzy and Napoleon during the disappearance of the statue cast on them the shadow of suspicion or, in other words, put someone on a wrong tack. Important questions bothered her:

"What kind of value could possibly comprise that cute bear statue in blue pants with a carrot in its pocket, and why did Gruben became so excited when it was stolen? Who snatched the bear and is there any connection with the theft of the paintings from the mega yacht, and what does Gruben actually know about all things?

Suzy made a decision to provoke Gruben's interest by throwing him bait. If, assuming that he somehow was connected to the theft and carried out his part of the job, but doesn't have knowledge of the entire operation, as it frequently happens. Through him one could come to his contacts and, possibly, track larger fish.

Finally, she looked at Napoleon, as if just noticing his presence.

"Napoleon, serious suspicions torment me."

"What's that?" asked Napoleon softly, still not letting her out of his sight and sensing impeding thunder.

"I suspect that Billy boy hides in his blue pants not only the carrot, but a big secret as well!" At that, she waved her index finger in the air, her beautiful ring with its huge stone gleaning.

"We have to admit the theft and ask for a price!"

Poor Napoleon, who was sipping his chocolate at the moment, choked, had a fit of coughing, and almost fell of his chair. He didn't want to believe his ears.

"Suzy, are you real? Do you understand what you just said? Where are you going to get that damned statue?" cried out Napoleon having his throat cleared already, but still breathless with excitement.

Suzy didn't reply immediately. She calmly and intently continued laying out her cards. Regretfully, Napoleon was well aware of her character, that if she took something in her head, there is no way to dissuade her.

Meantime, the squad more and more often started visiting the club cafeteria, taking their seats at a remote table and, leaning over it with an air of conspirators, lingeringly and enthusiastically whispered something to each other, simultaneously glancing covertly at the new female employee of the cafeteria, Jill Lee.

Suzy woke up early in the morning, threw on her soft pink robe, and thrust her feet into comfortable pink slippers in the shape of a hare's face with long ears. She took a seat by the table and laid out her cards. It was Wednesday and that meant there would be a Bingo game at the club house, and that she had to get her lab work done at the clinic. Her telephone rang. It was Napoleon. They agreed to meet at the clinic.

"Well, I believe there gonna be a meeting today," moving her cards from place to place on the table, she murmured. And she was not wrong. It was already dusk when Suzy drove up to the parking lot of the club house. She didn't have a chance to get out of her car, when another car with darkened glasses stopped close by. One of the windows came down, the door opened, and Gruben's head peeped out. He invited her into his car. She agreed.

"Hi, Suzy, how things are going?" asked Gruben.

"Pretty good, and you?"

"Suzy, where is the bear?" Gruben immediately came to business.

"Give it back."

"What would you care, and why are you so concerned about it?" Suzy asked in turn.

"Just to restore order and return it where it belongs."

"Yeah, sure, no doubts about that, but you see, the statue has big sentimental value to me and I don't feel like parting with it, not just yet."

"Suzy, don't be a fool, give it back."

"Well, it might cost you, Gruben"

"How much?"

"Let me think, taking into consideration maintenance expenses..." she drawled her words as if making calculations in her mind.

"Beast maintenance expenses, are you kidding?" in disbelief repeated Gruben.

"Suzy, there are people who are ready to pay a reasonable price."

"Okay, then, stop it here, and that's exactly with whom I am gonna negotiate!" and she cut him short.

"Very well, Suzy, but be careful. I warned you one more time." On that, their conversation was over. Suzy got out of his car and made her way to the club. She met her friends there and seemed to be very pleased with herself.

24 THE TRIP TO GEORGIA

The mountain heights sleep in the darkness of night
The quiet valleys are filled with a dewy haze.
The road has no dust, the leaves do not shake...

From Goethe (D. Smirnov-Sadovsky)

Judy inhaled a lungful of fresh, cool air, filled with the intoxicating fragrance of shrubs. Just as it was depicted on the painting, they found high giant mountains with permanent snow and glaciers covered tops that surrounded hilly green terrain. On one of the hills a stately construction was towered, a cathedral, erected in the fourteenth century. Judy immediately recognized it; however, no painting could ever relay or make you perceive that sensation of harmony between sweeping pristine nature and a magnificent creation of masterly skilled human hands, that inevitably evokes an exuberant feeling of genuine admiration.

Judy and Etienne arrived at the capital city of Georgia, Tbilisi, and checked in at the hotel, located on the main avenue and named after Georgian poet Shota Rustaveli. The next day they went to see some sights. The city, depicted by the Duke in his letters was hard to recognize. It was a modern European city, situated on the banks of a swift-flowing and insidious Mtkvari river, notorious for its rapids and vertiginous current. The city took pride in its high-rise buildings, shady green river walks, blooming parks and gardens, alleys, broad avenues, modern bridges, and great respect for its antiquities. The constructions with carved multicolored balconies, situated on hills, were preserved, and renovated, the Narikala Fortress as a symbol of city defense built in the fourth century overlooked the city and the river from the Mother of Georgia mountain reminding of a dramatic past of numerous rapacious invasions. Unchanged, however, remained the kindheartedness and hospitality of the Georgian people, the colorful folklore, and superb quality of Georgian food and wine. Judy and Etienne had a very intensive itinerary, however, and had to leave the very next morning in search of the cathedral, which they did. Driving their rental car through the picturesque landscape, they encountered mountains and hills covered with bright green vegetations, that contrasted pleasantly with the azure blue sky and some isolated white clouds drifting over all. Well-built countrymen houses, orchards, and vineyards were scattered over the hills. The local breed of cows, accustomed to the Georgian heat and hilly terrain, peacefully descended on rich ranges. Swift and cool mountain rivers, stumbling over sly rapids, swished in ravines. Amazingly, during their ride, they crossed several geographical zones from steppe to mountains with permanent snow and glaciers. The sights were impressive. By a winding mountain automobile road, they finally reached their destination and after parking their car, walked up to the cathedral on a stone paved path. The cathedral was open, and they went inside welcomed by one of the attendants. They looked around, trying to get adjusted to weak light. The interior of the cathedral was very simple. There were no fresco paintings, no plastering, and no electricity. Daylight barely penetrated through narrow windows. There were no other visitors, but here and there in front of Saint icons, thin yellowish candles were lit. Judy and Etienne walked around intently viewing walls, looking for a small niche with an icon inside, as depicted on the drawing. They had made already several rounds, but to no avail. Understandably, somewhat disappointed they headed to the exit. Right at the exit from the cathedral, however, they noticed a construction by the wall, apparently arranged at more recent times, that separated some space from the common hall and was, apparently, used as a utility room. Its wooden carved door happened to be ajar and approaching it they opened the door and went inside. They found themselves in an empty, but cozy, small room, all covered with rugs. There was an icon of George the Victorious on one of the walls, and under the icon flickering candles were placed on a small table. Between the table and the icon, a rectangular alcove in the wall was located. Judy pulled

104

out of her backpack her icon and tried to place it into the alcove. The icon slid easily inside it and seemed to fit perfectly. Suddenly, in front of their astonished eyes their icon started plunging down slowly into the wall, disappearing from their sight and, at the same time, something snapped right under their feet. They swiftly moved the rug they stood on, and under the rug emerged a massive metal ring of the wooden hatch. Etienne easily opened the hatch, under which they found a simple ladder with cross-bars, leading to the basement. They exchanged glances, as if saying "again underground" and it didn't take them long to decide what to do next. They both descended carefully to the basement holding cross-bars with both hands. Once underground, they lit it with their flashlights. Right there by the wall they found their icon. Picking up the icon and lightening their way with flashlights, they walked through a foot-worn narrow corridor, until they bumped into a wooden door, behind which they found a small quarter with icons and longtime extinguished candles. There were antique rugs on the stone flooring and walls, and the quarter looked like a monk's cell with its simple table, wooden bench, and wooden flat bed. On the table, though, they were surprised to find a photograph in a simple wooden frame. They started eyeing the photograph of a bridal couple, a tall handsome groom and a bride in white wedding gown with apparently expensive jewelry.

"Medallion!" involuntarily exclaimed Judy.

"Look, Etienne, our medallion is on the bride's neck." Absolutely, on the bride's neck there was beautiful medallion, very similar to the one they had in their possession. They carefully took the photograph out of the simple frame. On the reverse side of the photograph, as Judy expected, there was dedicatory inscription. It was a very tender inscription from the bride to her husband, and under the inscription a date.

"But wait, the date has different handwriting, and it doesn't look like a date at all. Something doesn't add up. This is no date. These, I believe, are geographical co-ordinates. Look." And she handed the photograph to Etienne.

"Yes, you're right! Okay, we will sort it out later."

Without losing much time, they thoroughly examined the small quarter. Behind a hanging rug, they found a hidden door with a metal sliding bolt.

The bolt was rusty, nonetheless, it would open easily. Not finding any-thing else noteworthy in the quarter, they took the photograph, and left the quarter through the hidden door entering another foot-worn narrow corridor lighting their way with flashlights. Soon, sounds of falling water reached them and gleams of light appeared. They hasten their steps and reached a widening that appeared to be a cave. On the opposite side to their entry into the cave, a waterfall roared, covering, or, to be more pre-cise, hiding another entrance into the cave. Using a narrow footpath lead-ing out of the cave and around the lake, they returned to the cathedral, which was still empty. They approached the carved wooden door, but this time it was locked.

Judy and Etienne left the cathedral, returned to their car, and shortly drove away. The next day, they set out to Paris. They needed to find out who were these people in the photograph and where the place, pointed by geographic coordinates, was located.

Regretfully, all the newspapers found in the Paris catacombs were lost, vanished along with unknown intruders. Nonetheless, in the library in Paris they were able to find some archived newspaper editions bound to-gether. Looking through them, they spotted a photograph of one of the famous jewelry exhibitions, where Duke Orlofsky was depicted with his famous tiara, Northern Lights, that evoked so much attention in the press that time. There they also found a description of his largest and purest diamond Polar Star, included in a tiara. Comparing the two photographs, they found that the groom on their photograph resembled Duke Orlofsky shown in the newspaper and assumed that the man on both photographs was Duke Orlofsky. However, who was the bride? This puzzle still needed to be worked out. They couldn't find any references regarding his marriage in the newspapers; however, some allusions were made about his dispatch to Caucasus right before the revolution in Russia. After that his trail went cold, nobody saw or hear from him again. Suppositions were made that he most probably had perished. Along with Duke Orlofsky van-ished his famous and richest jewelry collection, including the tiara North-ern Lights and the unique diamond Polar Star.

The dedicatory inscription on the back of the photograph and the date, made in a different handwriting, and, hence, presumably by different people, in truth turned out to be geographical coordinates that pointed to some islands in the Caribbean Sea, located close to the equator.

Regarding the islands, Judy, somehow, immediately got an idea. Undoubtedly, they are going to visit these islands as soon as possible. They could make the voyage on the yacht of one of her friends, Roger Hunter, a research scientist, enthusiastic seafarer, and explorer of the undersea world.

25 MANUEL

Judy returned from her trip to Georgia and Paris, bringing with her the photograph and the information uncovered with Etienne in the archives. She couldn't wait to show the photograph to her grandma. She arrived in Florida on a warm autumn evening and swiftly reached her house, finding grandma engaged in her favorite pastime, viewing family albums. Grandma loved viewing family albums and old photographs, that would bring back her memories, and she especially loved Judy joining her in her recollections. On arrival, Judy embraced her grandma's delicate body and kissed her warmly. She told her all about the exciting trip to Georgia, and about visiting the magnificent high-mountain cathedral, the photograph, and their findings in the Paris library. Grandma listened very attentively, took her magnifying glass and started viewing the photograph, Judy handed her, with interest.

"I can't believe it!" she exclaimed anxiously, almost immediately as she looked at the photograph.

"What a resemblance!" and she fussily started looking for something.

"What is it, grandma?" Judy asked her owlishly. Grandma, meantime, digging into old photographs, pulled out her mother Maria's wedding picture.

"Look," she said, laying both photographs side by side on the table with her still beautiful hands with thin, thinner than cigarette paper, and almost transparent white skin. Both brides wore beautiful white wedding gowns, looked of the same age, and strikingly resembled each other.

All of a sudden, grandma started recollecting something. It happened, that grandma's mother Maria had a twin sister Anna, but she doesn't know much about her besides that she passed away at a young age, and that they would never mention, or speak about her in the family. Judy took a thought. If suppose, that Duke Orlofsky was married to her great-grandmother's twin sister, Anna, then the mysteriousness and conspiracy around their marriage becomes quite understandable; it was due to the political situation in the country and a very real danger and threat of persecutions, chasings, and extermination of the family.

Thus, little by little, the curtain over the mysterious medallion started slightly to lift.

Judy parted with her grandmother and returned to her work in Los Angeles, full of good impressions and experiences, and quite pleased with the results of her investigations. Now, she had an expedition to the Caribbean islands to think about, and she definitively was looking forward to it.

Judy opened the chart of her new patient, and looked thoughtfully through the results of the investigations over and over again. Mr. Norman Dail, a 56-year-old patient, suffered from alcoholism. His repetitive periods of excessive alcohol consumption, invariably alternated with periods of abstinence. The initial alcohol consumptions, aimed to reduce strain in stressful situations, drink socially to keep company, or simply to indulge himself, over the years unnoticeably developed into addiction and he started consuming alcohol in large quantities that ultimately caused him alcoholism. As a heavy burden, alcoholism laid on his shoulders as well as on the shoulders of the folks deeply caring about him.

Pervasive consumption and the influence of high doses of alcohol on his body, and particularly, on his brain, caused it deep perturbations. Neuro-biological transformations in the brain, that initially had adaptive character in response to alcohol, later on themselves promote and maintain addiction, thus leading to irresistible and uncontrollable consumption, and, thereby, lock into the vicious circle. Escape from this vicious circle is very hard, but possible. Judy tried to understand what social factors could contribute to the development and maintenance of his addiction and what she could do to reduce their influence. Starting from his child-hood, she traced the evolvement of his personality to elaborate personal approach to his medical and psychological treatment. After she put to-gether her plan, and ordered him new investigations and treatment, she went to consult a few new patients, and then left the hospital.

Judy was well aware that her search for the richest jewelry collection that probably costs a lot of money, and to which she, most probably, has ancestral relationship, was not an easy matter. For this reason, she needed to analyze and discriminate what happenings around her could have direct relation to her search. In conjunction with this, she had questions about the rummaging in her house which emerged again with all seriousness.

"What was it, and what is hiding from her the squad?"
Judy headed to the club house where she had to apply make-up and dis-guise herself for the character. She also wanted to have a word with Suzy. Judy pinned up her hair and put on the wig with purple hair, then stuck on tattoos, put on a mini-skirt and pulled on high over-knee boots. After that, she stared at the mirror. Surprisingly, she couldn't recognize herself. Still, some requisites were missing, but she forgot them in the car, so she rushed to the parking lot where she noticed Suzy, who in a slow and dig-nified manner was extricating her plumpness out of the car. Judy imme-diately approached Suzy and, not even having a chance to open her mouth, she felt something cold and hard right under her chest.

"Get into the car without noise, quickly," she heard an unfamiliar voice saying. Judy obeyed and together with Suzy, got into the car with dark-ened windows that was parked right next to Suzy's. They both were blind-folded, and their hands were tied behind their backs. After driving a while, the car finally stopped, they got out and were walked somewhere. Upon arrival, their blindfold was loosened. It turned out to be some kind of huge warehouse with big boxes and wooden containers. Presently, they were approached by a short, thickset, and tanned man with black hair. He im-mediately came up to Suzy and put big sharp knife to her throat, slightly scratching her skin, leaking out some blood.

"Where is the bear, Suzy?"

"Who are you, and why do you ask for it?" Suzy returned recklessly.

"It's not of your business. Answer, where is the bear?"

"Take away your knife first, and untie our hands. We are not going to run away."

"Okay," he said, taking away his knife and untying their hands.

"Now tell me, where is the bear, and why did you steal it?"

"I don't know, and I didn't steal it." The knife glared in his hands again.

"I'm telling the truth. I didn't take the statue, but I would pay dearly to find out who did. I just do not understand why you are so concerned about it."

"Why should I believe you, and who is she?" He pointed at Judy.

"That's Jeanie, my trainee, a very talented one." Judy slowly swallowed her saliva and almost chocked on her chewing gum that she had forgotten she had in her mouth.

"Oh yeah, never heard of her."

"Excuse, me, talents like hers are not advertised, you know. Besides, I believe you had an expensive watch on your wrist not long ago. Check it out, you might find something exciting in her right high boot."

The surprised man looked at his empty wrist, then back to Suzy. Then, after that, he approached Judy and ordered her tug down her right boot. Judy, chewing her gum and averting his eyes, obediently and without a word tugged down her right boot, and handed it to the man. He carefully shook it over one of the boxes, and an expensive, gleaming, golden Rolex watch wheeled out of it. First, everybody froze, astounded with surprise and even lowered their weapons. Then, what seemed to be a grumble of admiration spread about. Obviously, talent like this took effect, and the man, growing softer, put his watch back on his wrist.

"I know her," announced a husky voice coming from somewhere behind them.

"Ray!" She recognized his voice immediately and grew cold all over.

"I know her, Manuel," repeated Ray now approaching them.

"Give them a chance, they might really help, besides, we can always kill them off."

"And just how are you going to help me?" The man, who was called Manuel, asked Suzy sarcastically.

111

"That's my business. I know people, but I need some time and, besides, it's gonna cost you."

"Be thankful if I let you go out of here in one piece," said Manuel angrily.

After a small discussion among themselves, the kidnappers blindfolded them again and took them to the car. Both were brought back to the parking lot and left there unhurt. When the kidnappers were already out of sight, Suzy got into the back seat of her car and with a gesture invited Judy to join her, simultaneously pressing her index finger to her lips. Somehow disconcerted, Judy questioningly looked at Suzy and followed her. Without a word Suzy slightly raised her blouse with a huge crochet flower on her bosom and Judy could see a recording device attached to her bra.

26 THE PROFESSOR

The weather was really lovely in Los Angeles. It was warm, but not hot yet. Judy took the elevator downstairs and stepped outside the building. The sun was shining in the blue, cloudless sky, and a soft breeze playfully and pleasantly was blowing her hair. Exposing face to the sun and gaily greeting her fellow workers and friends that she met on her way, Judy walked to another building where the cafeteria was located. On entering the cafeteria, she customarily took silver, placed it on her plastic tray, and headed for a buffet where in large pots and trays were laid out all kinds of food.

"Hi, Judy, how are you?" She heard a familiar voice and immediately turned her head.

"Oh, Roger, hi, haven't seen you for quite some time. Nice to see you again. I am fine, what about you?" she inquired, and at the same time chuckled to herself thinking— "the game leaves the den to look for the hunting man, and you are exactly whom I was looking for."

It was professor Roger Hunter, an enthusiastic scuba-diver, who is pursuing Medical and Biological research that concerns the influence of global warming on underwater life and coastal strip. Judy and professor Hunter had become acquainted at one of the scientific conferences a few years back. Both of them sincerely absorbed in science, very quickly found understanding, and became friendly and kept in touch. Occasionally, he would ask her for medical advice. As a prolific scientist he had registered a few inventions, that brought him good fortune. His recent invention represented an active component of medicine that was manu-factured from certain varieties of seaweed. The medicine presently was undergoing clinical trial. To conduct his research and seafaring, he had his own well-equipped and well-organized yacht, of which he was very proud.

They took their trays and seated themselves at one of the tables.

"Roger, I have some business to discuss with you; a serious one."

"Discuss serious business?" he repeated her words, looking at her with a somewhat barely perceptible smile, that Judy sensed right away. She was well aware, that her comely face, framed with thick, reddish, curly hair, which she always kept nicely done and her entire well-kept appear-ance very often shaded out her character and nature as a very knowledge-able, lettered, hard-working, consistent, and incredibly persistent in achieving her goals, person. The fact, oftentimes deeply upset her.

"But no, he couldn't possibly mean anything like that," she becalmed herself.

"Why not, why don't we meet somewhere next week and discuss your business," he responded willingly.

Judy always liked talking to Roger. First, he has always been very nat-ural. He could attentively listen and understand the other person, had a good sense of humor, and was well-read and well informed in many mat-ters. On the top of all these, he is athletically fit, has a pleasant smile, and broad shoulders. She simply liked him. She readily agreed to meet him next week in one of the cozy restaurants for dinner.

A few days passed without any special happenings, and after work Judy set off to meet Roger at the restaurant.

On meeting each other, they exchanged their greetings and took a ta-ble. Roger, noticed, by the way that she looked lovely in her little black dress and new hairdo.

"You look pretty handsome yourself," replied she.

After looking through the menu, they ordered their food and while waiting for it, Judy asked Roger about his work and upcoming expedi-tions. She pulled a map of the Caribbean Sea basin, out of her purse, and pointing out a spot asked him whether he knew anything about these is-lands, and could he possibly become interested in them for his research.

"As the matter of fact, yes. I've been thinking of exploring this region for quite some time now. You see, due to global warming, coral reefs are losing microscopic organisms, called zooxanthella and become discolored. Besides, there are endemic forms of sea stars there that I am very interested in at the present time. But why are you asking me these questions? Are you, too, taking interest in sea stars now?" Roger asked her quite surprised.

"Oh no, Roger. No, my interests are very far from sea stars," she replied.

"Then, what made these islands so attractive to you?"

"You see, Roger, to make long story short, it turned out that I am somehow related to a very rich Russian Duke Orlofsky, who vanished without a trace along with his world-famous jewelry collection right before the 1917 revolution in Russia. A persistent search for his collection by the former soviet government was unsuccessful. Nevertheless, just recently I received a message from him."

"A message from Duke Orlofsky, just recently?" not trying now to conceal his frank smile, repeated Roger.

"It is interesting. How did he relay it to you, by e-mail, or via messenger?"

"Oh, don't be sarcastic, it is serious," and she pulled out of her purse and put on the table in front of him the wedding photograph of Duke Orlofsky, that she had brought from Georgia.

"Beautiful couple," remarked Roger, "who are they?"

"We established it with Etienne, that the groom is presumably Duke Orlofsky himself, and about the bride, Judy slightly rubbed her forehead, there is supposition that she is the twin sister of my great-grandmother." Then, turning over the photograph, she pointed to the inscription.

"These are geographic coordinates, and they correspond to the group of islands of volcanic origin in Caribbean Sea. Knowing your special enthusiasm about volcanic islands and their coastal strip, I thought you might get interested in them as well and consider visiting them. In that case, Etienne and I could join you in the expedition."

A private company, created by Roger, was conducting research on the influence of global warming on underwater life and coastal strip. The

Company was so successful, that they even received governmental contracts. They also patented several ingredients of natural origin, that are used in modern drugs, and, naturally, bring the company big profits.

Roger, in his turn, asked Judy, "Who is Etienne?" Judy explained to him, that she and Etienne somehow are connected to each other through their family mystery and in short told him everything she knew. Roger listened to her very attentively and promised to give a thought to her proposition, and let her know about his decision as soon as possible. He also mentioned, that if he is to undertake this expedition to the islands, both Judy and Etienne should take part in the work along with his team. Judy naturally agreed. They spent a lovely evening chit-chatting and enjoying their meal.

In two weeks, Roger gave Judy a call and let her know, that he agrees to visit these islands, and that he will need a couple more weeks to organize and arrange all his affairs in Los Angeles.

Judy immediately gave a call to Etienne in Paris, and talked to Doctor van Bright about her vacation. Everything was working out nicely. Doctor Van Bright let her take a month vacation and Etienne was going to join them in Miami where the expedition would set sail to the islands.

27 THE EXPEDITION

On a warm spring Sunday morning, The Harmony, Roger's yacht, cast off from its Miami port according to a previously charted route. This was an expedition yacht trawler, fairly strong, and reliable, a sturdy vessel with large supply of water and combustible. A large part of the yacht was occupied with research equipment, nevertheless, the researchers' cabins were spacious and comfortable. Besides Roger, Judy, and Etienne, the team included five persons-- a woman research assistant, three men scuba divers, who also functioned as sailors, and Judy's nephew, Joseph, who besides being a talented computer guy, was also a very enthusiastic scuba diver and could be very helpful during the expedition.

Right from the beginning, good luck accompanied them. The weather was warm, the sea calm, and the wind favorable. For Judy, who had never before participated in a long sea navigation, the voyage and the anticipation of soon unraveling the family mystery, exerted a winy effect. However, on the fourth day of their navigation in the open sea, her elation had changed drastically and so did the weather. Clear blue sky became overcast, and the strong wind raised the sea. Suddenly an appalling storm broke out. However, Roger's team was an experienced and well-coordinated one in coping with the storm-tossed sea to keep the vessel safe. The tempest lasted for two days, pouncing immense waves upon the yacht, but on the third day the weather changed again as if by some magic. The sea became calm, and it felt like no storm had ever happened at all. The sky cleared of clouds and the sun started to shine, the wind subsided, and soon the contour of islands appeared ahead. Just as it was expected, these were a group of small islands. They came closer to one of them, and the dingy was launched into the water. The explorers, who approached the shore, detected a small, but quite deep, natural embayment surrounded by some precipitous cliffs that protected it from winds and storms, a place very suitable for the yacht to anchor. It was one of that amazing and picturesque places, created by nature. Before the cliffs a narrow strip of sand created beautiful beach. The Harmony entered the embayment and anchored.

Roger, with the ginger team, as they jokingly were named, Judy, Joseph, and Etienne, for they all were redheads, disembarked to the shore. Only now, when Judy saw Joseph and Etienne together similarly dressed in shorts, shirts and broad brim hat, she noticed how much they resembled each other. The team was ready for exploration and they started on the way finding a pass between cliffs. The part of the island they were exploring was densely covered with tropical vegetation, the other part bore traces of lava. The explorers moved further and further forward, finding traces of human constructions, and, now and then, they had to clear thick green vegetation, that hampered their advancement. The island seemed deserted by inhabitants most likely due to volcanic eruptions in near past. Soon, in front of them opened a cliffy terrain and a towered mountain. Meantime, they were approaching their destination point. It's here, Judy finally announced. They looked around, there was nothing but a cliff, that head off their way, so they took a good look at it. At a short distance from the ground, one could notice some cleft in it. It seemed that it was not hard to reach it, and they started to climb the cliff. Soon they reached the opening, which turned out to be much wider than they imagined it from below, and without difficulties they went inside it, one by one. As they advanced inside the opening, it grew wider and wider and, finally, brought them to the space between cliffs. They found themselves standing on the landing, that represented an overhang in the cliff, that befringed it. Carefully, following each other's steps without deviating an inch as Roger instructed them, they walked over a narrow overhang. Roger led the way, followed by Etienne, Judy, and Joseph, whom everybody considered absentminded and slightly outwardly, closing the rear. After walking some time in such an organized manner, they all of a sudden almost dashed against each other, as Roger unexpectedly came to halt, and even slightly backtracked. A very dangerous and venomous American lance-head snake, Bothrops, blocked their pass. Noticing the snake everybody froze on the spot. The snake, evidently somehow disturbed, meantime assumed a curved S shape and started vibrating its tail, that could mean only one thing; it was ready to attack. What to do? Wait and rely on its mercy, hoping that it would calm down and crawl away, or backtrack over the narrow pass, or jump from the high overhang? Its appearance, meantime, was becoming more and more dangerous and split seconds could determine their fate. However, in reality there was no other choice for them at the moment besides freezing motionless on the spot. The snake seemed to calm down and slowly started crawling in the opposite direction, but all of a sudden it turned around and was ready to lunge. At this very moment, an instrument that looked like a big gun gleamed in Roger's hand. Practically without taking aim he shot. A crackle sounded, scaring the snake away and a metal loop flashed like lightning in the air looping over the snake. The loop constricted the wringing body of the snake, advancing to its middle. Along with the loop, a collapsible metal hinge was shot out, that held the loop and kept the snake on certain distance. He deftly hooked the snake, slightly lifting it from the ground, slipped the snake from the overhang and loosened the loop. That instrument was devised by Roger himself and in many occasions rendered him invaluable assistance saving his life. The danger had passed, everybody had a sigh of relief, and they continued on their way. After walking some distance, they found themselves at the entrance into the cave. Lighting their way with flashlights, they entered the deep cave, now closely watching their steps and looking around. No sooner had they found a narrow pass inside the cave and followed it, than Roger, who was still leading the way, suddenly paused listening attentively. He lifted his hand and gestured everybody to stop and get silent. Everybody immediately froze silent and pricked up ears. Human voices reached them from some distance ahead. Roger, Judy, and Etienne carefully sneaked behind a heap of stones, that happened to be there. Before their astonished eyesight opened a chamber, reminiscent of a habitable room with a roughly hammered table and chairs. A man, sitting by the table was engrossed in looking through and examining some of multiple papers laid over in front of him, constantly adjusting glasses on his nasal bridge. Besides him there were two other men armed with machine guns. Sitting by the table was a man that strongly reminded Judy of someone. She strained her memory.

"Centauries!" Almost cried the astonished Judy, covering her mouse with palm of her hand.

"Of course, Centauries, but how on earth did he get here, and what is he doing in this cave?" Centauries, meantime wrapped his hands around his head and anxiously cried out,

"A planet, a planet, who could possible imagine, everything adds up, everything in agreement!"

Finally, Centauries raked together all papers laid on the table, and along with others went away disappearing from the caves in the opposite direction. With one hand he was pressing the papers to his breast, and with the other one waving in the air as if he was amazed with something. Evidently, there was another entrance into the cave. When the voices died out, Roger gestured to the others and everybody came out of hiding. It was necessary to find out who were they, what they are doing on the island, and why they are armed with machine guns. Trying not to make any noise, Roger and the others followed the strangers in a narrow tortuous corridor that lead from the chamber. Soon gleams of light appeared and a strange noise started reaching them. They came out to the light and, hiding themselves behind the shoulder of the cliff, searched for the origin of the strange noise. Below, at the foot of the mountain, on a sandy landing, a helicopter ready to take to the air was waiting for the strangers. Roger and ginger team were observing their every move. Soon Centauries and his armed men got aboard the helicopter and it took off the ground heading to one of the nearby islands and shaded from the view. Roger, with the ginger team, returned to the chamber that somehow looked like a research lab. Judy looked about; the chamber reminded her of something. She has already seen it. A massive roughly built table, and some likeness of chairs around it, papers on the table. Apparently, Etienne had similar perceptions and he started attentively examining the interior of the cave. He paused in front of one of the walls because he noticed a niche, by shape and size resembling niche in Georgian cathedral. There was a long-time extinguished candle in a simple candle holder inside it. He carefully checked the niche, it had regular square shape, its walls were very smooth, and there was no doubt it was created by human hands. However, it was unknown whether it hid a concealed mechanism or not. They could only check it with their icon, that was left on the yacht. Thus, they would have to go back to the yacht and bring the icon with them. After careful inspection of the chamber and not finding anything else of particular interest, they returned to the yacht with a firm resolution to come back on the following day and continue their exploration.

The next day Roger, Judy, Joseph, and Etienne easily reached the chamber bringing with them their icon. When Etienne tried to place the icon inside the niche, they matched each other perfectly. No sooner he placed the icon into the niche than a boulder at one of the walls started to move, opening behind it an entrance and a stone stairway, leading upward. They all went inside and started climbing up the stone serpentine that brought them to the top of the mountain. Here, they found a well-preserved structure, that looked like an observatory. They thoroughly inspected the observatory and found a telescope, some notes, and an icon exact copy of the one they had in their possession. Upon completing their exploration and collecting the new icon, notes and stellar cards, they went down. To their surprise the entrance to the stair was closed again, and a similar niche inside the boulder was empty. Etienne placed inside it the newly found icon, and the boulder moved again letting them out. On the other side of the boulder inside the niche there now appeared two identical icons. They collected both icons and returned to the yacht.

On the yacht, Judy and Etienne looked through the papers, that turned out to be astronomical cards and notes. They also compared the two icons, that appeared completely identical. Using a tiny pipe, Etienne opened up the new one, to find there behind the icon, a carefully folded sheet of paper with some mysterious blueprint. The blueprint was very detailed and one of the rooms was marked with a cross. As they found out later, the building turned out to be a University, built in the last century by the initiative and means of one of the Jesuit monks and is located in Brazil. Thus, new hopes and a new itinerary, this time to Brazil, emerged in front of Judy and Etienne. Will they finally unravel the mystery of their medallion, Duke Orlofsky, and his vanished famous jewelry collection? It is hard to say.

After finishing the exploration of the cave, Judy, Joseph, and Etienne completely submersed into the work of Roger's expedition. The weather was good and the sea calm. The scuba-divers made multiple photographs and collected exceptional samples for research. The expedition was very successful and Roger was very pleased with the results. The aims of the expedition were fulfilled and it was time to return. Nonetheless, unanswered question remained. Who were these armed strangers in the cave, and what they were doing on the deserted island? Especially intriguing was to find out what Centauries has to do with them? Exploration of nearby islands this time was not in their plans and, in spite of remained unanswered questions, The Harmony was returning to Miami.

28 THE RETURN

The Harmony returned to Miami port without any complications. Roger was very pleased with the results, that exceeded all his expectations. They collected unique samples for further investigation and made multiple photographs. Judy always liked Roger and related to him with deep respect, but the expedition and the research they conducted together let them get to know each other better and, in a friendly way, brought them closer. The success of the expedition to a great extent was predetermined by the organized and coordinated team, where everyone brought their special talent, gift, and ability, persistence and task-oriented work. Judy and Etienne, in turn, advanced in their search and got closer to solving their mystery. After completion of the expedition, Etienne returned to Paris. The blueprint, hidden in the new icon that happened to be an exact copy of the one Judy had previously found in her great-grandmother's trunk, remained with Judy. They resolved to coordinate all their further steps and make a trip to Brazil as soon as possible and as an opportunity allows them to do so.

Judy returned to Los Angeles and got back to work. Naturally, a whirlpool of hospital life and new patients completely absorbed her attention. On her return, Judy related to Doctor Van Bright all about her findings on the island and about the unexpected encounter there of Centauries in the company of armed strangers. As usually, Doctor Van Bright listened to her keenly and, not surprisingly, the episode with Centauries and armed men evoked his special attention.

"By what chance Centauries landed on that island, who would have thought of it. What a surprising entwinement. I wonder, where is he now, has he returned to Los Angeles, and who were these armed men? An important question rises immediately, whether he was there by his own will or under constrain, and what they all could possibly do on the deserted island? Have you got any assumptions, Judy?" Judy pondered over his questions trying to picture it again what she had witnessed in the island. Strangely enough, neither that time, nor now had she any impression that Centauries was kept under any pressure or constraint. As a matter of fact, completely on the contrary. As judged by the intonation of their voices reaching her in the cave, and observation of the armed men's behavior from the far, Centauries was with them on friendly terms, engaged in a lively conversation. Judy shared her perceptions with Doctor Van Bright.

"Tell me, Judy, could Centauries somehow recognize you or simply see you there. This is very important."

"I don't think so," she confidently replied. "Over the course of the entire expedition the helicopter never made another appearance and even if the expedition was noticed, there were no attempts to obstruct our work or contact us. It's worth noting, by the way, that the expedition came to be very successful."

"I am very glad to hear that, and especially that you're safely back. I am sure your patients missed you greatly. Now, regarding your medallion, what are you going to do next? Do you have any plans for the future in the works already?"

"Oh, sure! At the first opportunity, we are going to visit that University in Brazil, hoping finally to solve our mystery."

"Well, good luck with that."

"Doctor Van Bright, what about the murder investigation? Any news?" Judy asked him in her turn.

"Investigation," pensively he repeated.

"I do not have track of any new details just yet, however, it looks like the things are taking an unexpected turn and I want you to meet Steven. He might take an interest in your observations on the island."

"Sure, any time," she immediately agreed, asking him at this point to bring along her nephew, Joseph, who turned out to be very helpful for the expedition and could have noticed some details she missed. Doctor Van Bright appeared to like the idea, and they agreed to meet Steven at Doctor Van Bright's villa in the evening.

Judy thanked Doctor Van Bright for his interest in her search, left his office, and headed to her patients. She also needed to meet Suzy and find out what's new and what they are still hiding from her.

It has to be said that bringing into the case Doctor Van Bright, of his cousin Doctor Mark Van Bright, and his son Steven, who presently held high a position in Los Angeles police, took immediate effect and brought results. Especially fruitful was the involvement of Steven's son, a young and very talented detective, Brian Van Bright. The entire troupe had been scrupulously investigated and it was found out that the vanished actor happened to be an engineer, working at one of the high technology enterprises. Immediately a warrant was obtained to search his house. However, they were late, someone had already paid him a visit looking for something. The questions immediately were raised, who were they, what they were looking for, and did they find it or not?

Brian, a very astute young man, an enthusiastic sportsman, and a former captain of the winning high school volleyball team had one other passionate hobby. Besides sports, Brian loved antiques and especially furniture and puzzles or mystery boxes. One of his first mystery boxes Brian received as a birthday gift from his grandfather Doctor Mark Van Bright. The mischievous boy had to spend a few days in the hospital due to fracturing his leg that coincided with his fifth birthday. The box pulled his attention then and after that they became his passion. He could spend hours trying to disclose their secrets, taking them apart and putting them back together again. This passion will render him a valuable service in the case of the vanished engineer, whose house search was unsuccessful at the beginning. However, in the engineer's study, Brian immediately noticed an antique French desk, a magnificent piece of work. By experience Brian knew that desks like this often times harbor secret compartments that for an unknowing person is practically impossible to detect. Brien approached the desk with curiosity and started carefully opening drawers and sliding them back into place, simultaneously thoroughly pal-pating them. The desk happened to be in a very good condition, all its parts were original ones. He was working and puffing over it, and in doing so earned wry and ironic glances of his colleagues. However, in less than half an hour everybody heard his exciting cry "Bingo!" After all, he was not wrong; the desk really contained a secret compartment and he man-aged to reach and open it. Out of that compartment, Brien triumphantly pulled out the engineer's computer. Now they needed to break into it and check out his files. The computer was brought to the research lab, where they tried to reach its files. However, the task at hand proved to be a very challenging one and, no matter how hard they tried, they were unable to open his files. Even famous hackers, invited kindly for the occasion, were unable to help.

Steven, immersed in his thoughts, was pacing back and forth in front of his desk, his hands clasped behind his back. The case he reluctantly got involved in upon the insistence of his uncle Doctor Kristopher Van Bright and which at the beginning seemed to be some kind of unreal fantastic tale, gradually acquired a very real outline. Steven tried to summarize; what was known at the present time? As alleged by Doctor Van Bright, a murder was committed at the clubhouse during the theatrical perfor-mance, but the body had disappeared without a trace, which by itself raised doubts. Thorough investigation of the troupe, however, revealed that one of the actors, an engineer, working in one of the private high-tech enterprises had vanished, and had not returned from his unscheduled vo-cation. What is it a mere coincidence or are these incidents linked to each other? Furthermore, someone had searched the engineer's house before they could. Investigation of the engineer's financial records, his contacts, and talking to his girlfriend and coworkers did not reveal anything partic-ular or suspicious. According to them, he was very dedicated to his work and a harmless person. Besides, his girlfriend was quite surprised that he had gone to the Bahamas without letting her know, which was completely out of his character.

Brian, nevertheless, was able to find out that someone really set out to the Bahamas under the engineer's name, however, nobody had seen or heard from him since. He seemed to have vanished into thin air. The engineer's computer, so safely hidden from an uninvited intruder's eyes, could contain important additional information, but they were unable to penetrate his files. Steven paused, quit measuring his office with his footsteps, and took a seat by the desk. At that moment, his telephone rang. Doctor Van Bright was calling to let him know that Judy has returned from the expedition and that she has a story he might be very interested in. So, he's inviting Steven to his villa in the evening to meet her and her nephew, Joseph, to have a conversation. Steven agreed.

Upon return from the expedition, Roger had offered Joseph a position in his company. Joseph, thanks to his diverse knowledge, audacity, and perseverance in achieving goals, along with his expertise as a computer guy, blended seamlessly into Roger's team and proved to be very useful. He reflected on the offer and meantime resolved to stay with Judy for a few weeks.

In the evening, after work, Judy and Joseph set off to Doctor Van Bright's villa, where they met Steven and Brian. Judy related to Steven her story about the successful expedition to the island, and, naturally, mentioned her surprising sight of Centauries, accompanied by armed men. As Doctor Van Bright anticipated, Steven immediately took very close interest in Judy's story and started asking her multiple questions. How did they look, what they were talking about, did she hear any snatches of conversation? However, at that time Judy, was completely engrossed by Centauries trying to ascertain for herself, was it really Centauries, or someone that simply resembled him? Besides, all the armed men wore military style khaki with berets covering their heads so she couldn't get good look at them.

However, Joseph, whom everybody considered absentminded and slightly "outwardly," in reality was very observant. Furthermore, he never parted with his binoculars that hung on his neck, because he loved watching birds with it.

"On the wrist of one of the 'green men,' that's how he called armed man, gleamed a beautiful watch," he recalled.

"A watch!" The incident with Suzy immediately bubbled to the surface and she started to rack her brain.

"Manuel, that was the name of the man with the beautiful Rolex watch. Was it the same Manuel and the same Rolex watch?" No, she couldn't answer this question, no matter how hard she tried, but she told Steven everything about the incident with Suzy.

"Now, is this not too many coincidences?" she thought to herself.

With that, Judy didn't miss an opportunity to tell everybody how helpful was the participation of Joseph in the expedition; and she proudly described him as a virtuoso-computernik, who from his childhood was absorbed in computer programming, and was a repeat winner of international mathematical competitions.

A virtuoso-computernik! Steven immediately perked up his ears. That's exactly what he needed right now.

"You never know, 'When the good lord looks away, then the evil one starts to play,'" thought Steven and decided to give it a shot. He invited Joseph to his Lab to try to break in into engineer's computer and reach his files.

The next morning Joseph arrived at the Lab, where he was given a badge, and he modestly entered the hall. He took a seat by the computer, and before his long fingers started snapping over the key board, he adjusted the badge hanging on his neck and slightly pushed his glasses on his nasal bridge. Almost immediately, file after file started flickering on the monitor; and the lab personnel grew besides themselves with joy. However, their joy melted away very soon when they encountered a file marked as *Secret*. The content of this file struck them as thunder. It contained schemas, graphs, and formulas that had no relation to his work whatsoever, and which he shouldn't access. Nonetheless, the information was encrypted in his computer. How on earth he could get all this information and where is he now? Is there any connection between the vanished engineer, his secret file, and the murder that took place at the club house? As doctor Van Bright insisted, an actor or someone disguised as an actor, was dead. He was absolutely positive about it. Then where is the body, and how it could disappear without any trace? Thorough investigation of the murder scene could not reveal any clues, no trace of blood was found at that time, and the decorations burned in the fire that took place in the storage facility, soon afterwards.

One thing was absolutely clear, that the computer of the engineer somehow contained information suggestive of scientific and industrial espionage. How did he obtain all this information and what he was going to do with it? Did he have accomplices? All these things had to be found out.

If assuming that Doctor Van Bright was right and the murder really took place, the murder victim could be the engineer. Was he himself involved in espionage or had the information fallen into his hands by chance? The latter possibility couldn't be ruled out and, in fact, could cost him his life. If the information had fallen to him by chance, then whom was it meant for?

Now, regarding Centauries, Steven thoroughly questioned Judy about the episode with him. Immediately lots of questions arose in his mind: was he under any constraint on the island, who were these armed men, what they were doing there, and what interest they could possibly take in Centauries? Centauries, who suffered from Bipolar disorder and worked at one of the private high-tech companies before his diagnosis, was regarded as an excellent computer specialist, had a contradictory nature, and was seriously absorbed by Astronomy. Which one of his qualities attracted them, and where was Centauries now? There were a multitude of questions, awaiting clarification. What did Centauries and the engineer have in common? They both were participants of Doctor Van Bright's experimental troupe, and from time to time received treatment and observation in the psychiatric clinic. The experimental theatrical troupe, created under the initiative of Doctor Van Bright, was very popular. The road tours and performances were conducted all over the country and hundreds of people were involved. Although the very notion of such a troupe was subjected to constant attacks from the Medical community, and especially Doctor Van Bright's ill-wishers, patient treatment results, however, were very impressive and spoke for themselves.

29 THE EVENTS OF THE PAST

The death of his beloved Duchess Anna, expulsion to Caucasus, and the breaking up with his folks made the grieving Duke Orlofsky disengage from the worldly life, leave the ancient city of Tiflis, and settle down in one of the reclusive high-mountain monasteries in Georgia where he resigned himself to meditations and ruminations. Nonetheless, fresh mountain air, the breath-taking and untouched beauties of nature, the very special warmheartedness and soulfulness of local people, had on him a very beneficial influence. However, alarming pieces of news reaching him from Petrograd exerted a more and more sobering effect on him. The events in Petrograd developed swiftly. After the February unrest in the capital, revolution actually had happened, and the monarchy fell. The royal family was arrested and sent to exile. Any attempts of the Duke to somehow exert his influence on the course of events from afar were not successful. The subsequent take-over by Bolsheviks in October 1917 and the sweeping all country violence and bloodshed convinced Duke Orlofsky to abandon his country, depart abroad, and rescue his children, who undoubtedly were in grave danger.

A tap on the door of a modest monastic cell where Duke Orlofsky was sitting by a simple desk, diverted his attention from the papers and thoughts, in which he was deeply submersed, to a monk who appeared on the threshold.

"Petre, batono," which in translation from the Georgian language means Mister Peter,

"You have a visitor."

"Awaiting, awaiting, impatiently awaiting, let him in!" said the Duke moving papers aside and rising from the table to meet his visitor. At that moment, a tall handsome young man with a pale white face, black curly hair, and expressive dark eyes, outlined by dark eyebrows, entered the cell. His entire appearance radiated courage and nobility. He was dressed in black Georgian traditional clothing with tight high leather boots and a belted sword.

"Goga, at last! Extremely glad to see you!" After shaking their hands and embracing each other, they took seats by the table. Unnoticeably, a monk sneaked inside the cell and laid on the table a decanter filled with wine, glasses, and some food. The visitor with a pale face, immediately got down to business without touching the food.

"I have good news from the North, Peter. We were able to find people sympathetic to the family, who are ready to do everything necessary to help with your plan. Local authorities, so far, do not suspect anything about the twins since along with Duchess Anna, a child, who died in the village was buried as her only newborn daughter. The twins, along with Elizaveta, Klavdiya, and Shurochka immediately were taken away to another county by Maria, who recently delivered a baby herself. According to plan, Elizaveta will bring your twins to the pier, where she will be met by Madam Clementine Leblanc, who will be dressed as a sister of mercy with the red cross. She will take up the twins from Elizaveta as orphans intended for an orphanage. The plan is already in action, and soon we can anticipate news from them.

"This is all good, but is Elizaveta up to such a difficult task? After all, she's just a kid herself, and will have to cross three harsh northern rivers with the precious load," pensively asked the Duke.

"I believe she is. Besides, there will be eyes on her at all times and, if necessary, she will be assisted," replied Goga.

"Help us, God." The Duke cordially thanked his devoted childhood friend, George Badiani, who also was related to him from his maternal lineage.

Little time was left before the departure abroad, and the Duke had also to take care of his famous jewelry collection. No doubts that his collection and he himself were subjects of close interest for the new Russian authorities. Part of the collection had been delivered to the Paris international exhibition and left there for further instructions before the revolution. To his knowledge, an unhealthy interest has been already manifested by the new Russian government.

A smart and nimble girl, Elizaveta, as expected, coped with the task, but she brought only the boy since the twin girl fell very ill and would not be able to endure the trip. Elizaveta crossed three Northern rivers and delivered the live and healthy child to the pier, where she was met at a pre-arranged place by a Sister of Mercy, who took the child from her and boarded the ship. Thus, the twin children were separated. The boy subsequently was taken out of the country by Madam Clementine Leblanc, a former governess of one of the high-ranking families in Petersburg, and the girl, whose recovery nobody could believe, survived and was left in Russia with her auntie, who raised her as her own child. Persecutions, Red terror, and extermination of high social groups that followed the Bolshevik coup, made it dangerous and practically impossible not only to smuggle the twin girl away from the country, but even attempts to make inquiries about her.

Madam Clementine Leblanc successfully took the twin brother to France, where she placed him according to Duke Orlofsky's instructions in one of the monasteries near Paris as an orphan under an assumed French name.

Thus, separated in very early childhood, the twin brother and sister never suspected each other's existence and eventually will come to live in different countries and, subsequently, their descendants will even live on different continents.

Being an intelligent, well-educated person, fluently speaking several foreign languages, Duke Orlofsky hid his children from the new Russian Authorities and saved their lives. Furthermore, he managed to vanish from the country without a trace, taking away with him his precious jewelry collection, which was the subject of unabated pursuit by the Soviet government.

The Duke, however, didn't stay in France for long. Having left his son at the monastery near Paris allowing his stay and education and, himself joining the Jesuit Order under the name of Father Bernard, he left for Brazil.

A group of fourteen strong athletic men were energetically cutting their way with machetes through the thick shrubby rainforest. A few miles were still left before a rest stop, but the tiredness of the people and loaded animals after having covered the difficult road started to have an effect.

The expedition, headed by Father Bernard, and also included his friends, an honorable family of rich plantation owners and, at the same time rapt explorers of the wilderness, brothers Antonio, Diego, and Juan de Sanchez. They were contemplating exploration of the land as suitable for expansion of their coffee plantation, building of the railroad, and exploration of a river for the possibility of ferrying crops and goods.

The brothers De Sanchez were explorers by vocation and devotedly loved their country, dreaming of the development of new lands and making them suitable for agriculture. When Farther Bernard spelled out his plan of expedition for them, they met it enthusiastically and agreed not only to finance it, but personally take part in it.

The way of the courageous explorers led through the rainforests full of wild animals, waylaying them everywhere, on the land and on the tree branches. These were: stealthy jaguars, sneaking up, pumas, most venomous snakes, and, of course, deadly insects, that transmitted severe diseases like malaria and yellow fever. An estimated up to 70,000 species of mosquito, horse-flies, and wasps relentlessly strayed about them every day. No less dangerous were tribes of local aggressive Indians, that followed them at all times, and considered any intrusion to their forests as infringement upon their land and hence oftentimes displayed particular cruelty and aggression.

Nevertheless, the well-equipped, organized, and experienced expedition, despite being small in number, successfully was advancing to its goal, surmounting all the difficulties and danger that cropped up along the way, without losses. They finally reached the river. Exploration of a stretch of the river bed for possible future navigation and crop fretting, needless to say, was bringing additional difficulties and danger for the explorers, as they were trusting themselves to unknown water flow with its inherent rapids, gyrating current, and cataracts, not mentioning perilous inhabitants of the waters such as anacondas, crocodiles, and flesh-eating fish among others. Thereupon, how not to call to memory the courageous and fearless exploration of the uncharted before, insidiously unpredictable and treacherous river of Doubt, undertaken by the American President Theodore Roosevelt. That journey inspired explorers and bolstered their confidence in success.

Early in the morning, after a brief rest and sleep, all preparations for further advancement by the river commenced. Their canoes loaded with life-sustaining essentials, and suited for heavy cargo, were launched to the water. All preparations were wrapped up, and explorers took their places in canoes. No sooner had their paddles hit the water, when light arrows poisoned with curare, started whistling all around them, striking paddles and nearly missing travelers. Thus, the commencement of descent on the river was marked by the first manifestation of Indian animosity. Now, one could expect from them more hostile actions.

The canoes, built by design of Father Bernard himself, turned out to be light, and, at the same time, of good quality, and easily maneuverable. Their buoyancy well displayed itself at the fist rapids and cataracts they encountered, which were overcame with ease. Nevertheless, further down the river they could encounter more serious obstacles and testing.

By the end of the day, after the prolonged descent on the river, the expedition found a suitable place for their overnight halt and made a landing. The hammocks were hanged, and the supper prepared. The nightfall contributed to the tired travelers its own peculiar exotic, as the danger around them, that manifesting itself by harrowing cries of night animals, became invisible. Nevertheless, the exhausted travelers were overcome by sleep. Their rest, however, didn't last long. Strange sounds reached them in their sleep, bellicose cries, songs, and dances. A tribe of the local Indians with colorful makeup, garnished with feathers on their heads and no clothes, surrounded the expedition. Hurried by menacing cries and songs, the explorers swiftly woke up, packed up, took aboard their canoes, and, without pre-testing of the waterway ahead of them, hastily went away. The Indians began chasing them in their clumsy dugouts. All of a sudden, the stream alarmingly speeds up and, before anybody realized impeding danger, their canoes plunged into a water fall. In a twinkle of an eye, everybody wound up in the water. The current was swift and the matter was complicated by churning water that threatened to engulf everybody and everything. Hitting his head against a boulder, Father Bernard fell unconscious and a few minutes separated him from being completely and forever engulfed by the river. At this very instant a resilient body with long black hair dived unnoticed into the water and tanned hands as strong as a pair of pincers grasped the body of Father Bernard.

When Father Bernard came to by the campfire, his companion fellow travelers were around him. Even some of their inventory, including canoes, had survived. Nobody could really explain how they all made it out of the water. The puzzle, however, was puzzled out very soon. Taking a view at each other, they noticed a half-naked stranger, sitting around the camp fire and smoking a pipe. A young Indian was observing the travelers slowly coming to. "Mongo," announced he proudly, poking himself in a chest, when ascertained that he was noticed. After that the expedition was reinforced by a new member. Mongo was an admixture of Indian and a white woman and as an accidental bystander, he had witnessed everything that was going on. Answering the call of the blood, he would return to the rainforest once in a while to immerse himself into the elements of his ancestors. He had rescued Father Bernard from an imminent death and helped other members of the expedition swim ashore. Mongo turn out to be a very strong young fellow, smart, and familiar with the surroundings. He continued the descent on the river with the expedition and was indispensable in negotiations with local tribes attempting to explain to them their good intentions that didn't, however, alleviate tribal hostility.

Upon completion of the expedition at the risk of their lives, the purpose was achieved-- they explored new land and determined the possibility of navigation on certain stretches of the river band. Between Father Bernard and Mongo, a strong friendship sprang up. The young fellow, whose initial schooling was carried on by his mother, appeared to be very bright and eager to learn. Father Bernard in every way supported his education. However, Mongo's expeditions into the perilous rainforest didn't stop and during one of his trips he contracted a severe form of malaria. Father Bernard took the young man into his care and cured him with

"Jesuit powder." His young and strong body coped with illness and recovered. Mongo showed special interest in the stars. He would spend hours looking at the starry sky using unsophisticated devices; he also transferred his passion to Father Bernard.

The expansion of coffee plantations and exploration of new ways of fretting the crop, gave plantation owners great advantage and brought to them and to Father Bernard, large gains and profit. Father Bernard, in his turn, financed the building of a university, and, later on, an observatory on one of the islands in the Caribbean Sea. The building place for the observatory was chosen by Mongo as a best point for observation of certain celestial bodies. However, a volcanic eruption that occurred destroyed the observatory and a large part of the small island, and forced inhabitants to abandon it.

30 THE EXTREMELY AMBITIOUS PLANS
OF THE CRIMINAL ENTERPRISE

The FBI, meantime, was working on revealing a criminal chain of drug traffickers, that was under control by a Criminal Enterprise successfully operating on the West as well as on the East coasts. One of the criminal enterprise strongmen was Manuel, who, as it was known, had a great passion for expensive watches. The FBI managed to introduce undercover agents into the chain. However, it is one thing to reveal a criminal chain, and the other is to pull it all out and bring it to justice. They needed facts, witnesses, and proofs of committed crimes.

Due to Grand Jubilee—a tricentennial celebration of the foundation of one of the cities on the East coast, whose name includes the word bear, a batch of bear statues, created in Mexico on the border with California, was underway to the East coast, where they would be installed.

Drug traffickers, who resort to all kind of devious means to smuggle and spread drugs, resolved to take advantage of the situation and substitute one of the bear statues and load it with cocaine. As the matter of fact, the whole statue was made of a special mixture of cocaine, that could be released and purified by chemical reaction. Unhampered, the bear statues were delivered to the warehouse of the city on the East coast, where the particular bear would be substituted again for a real one. However, the project went sour. Due to an approaching high category hurricane and impeding disastrous flooding, that was truthfully predicted and impeccably and painstakingly forecast by all the local TV channels, the delivered

137

bear statues were unexpectedly and urgently moved to a new location. After the hurricane, which fortunately and drastically lost its strength right upon arrival and landfall, the bears were immediately mounted on pedestals. At the same time, the FBI, having information that the Farmers Bear statue contained a large batch of drugs, for the purpose not to permit its distribution through the city, brought it into "requisition" and substituted the statue before it was mounted in place. The theft of the innocent Farmers Bear Billy in blue pants and carrot in his pocket in broad daylight and in plain view, was intentionally arranged to coincide with the arrival of the great thievish authority in the past, Suzy and her inseparable friend and accomplice of many years, Napoleon.

The disappearance of the bear statue made quite a stir and was meant to throw criminals off the scent.

The theft of the statue deeply shocked the Enterprise, suspecting now rival grouping and Suzy, who was either used by rivals, or acted out of her own personal incentives. In either case, they needed to have a talk with her. That's why she was abducted along with the completely unsuspecting Judy, being in the wrong place and wrong time. Manuel, who was so concerned and interested in the statue, personally attended their meeting with Suzy and, perhaps, that was one of the desirable consequences of the FBI operation.

Suzy's assurances that she had nothing to do with the theft didn't convinced him and for this reason she was under constant close surveillance. Manuel also couldn't rule out that it was the work of a rival group that had simply used Suzy's presence in the city to make him follow a false track. As the matter of fact, Suzy and her entourage were under surveillance for a long time. That's why their houses were searched, but nothing had been found there.

The surprising and inexplicable appearances of Ray in very critical situations of Judy's life, was astonishing for her. Convincing Manuel to give Suzy a chance to get on the trail of a thief saved them both lives, not mentioning his timely assistance in the Paris catacombs. At the same time, though, she didn't forget that stressful "Vampire Ball," which also demanded explanation.

If that was really Manuel in company with Centauries on the island, it could mean only one thing, that some of the troupe members, who freely travel along with decorations all over the country, could be involved with a criminal chain of drug traffickers. The detection of the secret information concerning National Security in the engineer's computer further complicated the matter since financing of industrial and scientific espionage by a Criminal Enterprise couldn't be ruled out.

Steven was well aware now that the case, that had started as some kind of fantasy, in reality was a very serious matter and, in his turn, without any delay, informed a concerned superior organization.

Receiving new information about possible financing of industrial and scientific espionage by the Criminal Enterprise, the FBI immediately took up the lead to find out where the information could have leaked from. They tracked dates and places of common meeting points, how the engineer could obtain the information, and who and how could use it.

The experts and scientists came to the conclusion that the information found in the engineer's computer, is concerned with a new type of engine. The development of a new crystalline alloy that in the void of space and under the influence of cosmic rays to which it is very sensitive, transforms and changes its three-dimensional structure. On speeding up to high velocity, crystal qualities and characteristics reverse and assume their original structure releasing in the process immense energy, that could be used in a new type of engine for space crafts. Notably, that the engine, due to new crystal technology could be very light and compact. To regain consumed energy, a space craft will need to slow down. On a certain velocity, the process of energy replenishment resumes. For whom would such information be intended and how they were going to use it?

Centauries, a talented computer engineer, mathematician, and amateur astronomer with a quick-temper, intolerant to objections, was underestimated in one of the high technology companies, and lost his favorite job. As a consequence, he fell ill. What made him interlace with a Criminal Enterprise, and which of his qualities and expertise had criminals found useful for them? What were they up to?

The information obtained from Steven and Judy turned out to be a significant contribution to the case. Prompt and intent observation commenced over the group of islands in the Caribbean Sea using satellite assistance and, indeed, a suspicious activity was noticed on one of them. To further investigate the matter, the FBI decided to intrude into the region under the cover of a new scientific research expedition.

Although a detailed investigation of ambitious cosmic plans of the Criminal Enterprise are beyond present narration and will be scrupulously addressed later on, leaping ahead it may be said that they planned to gain control over the Earth by means of cosmic piracy. The Criminal Enterprise also had a stab at reclamation of one of the planets of the Solar system for digging rare metals and minerals for creation of the before mentioned special engine. To conduct necessary research investigations, the Enterprise assembled a group of "outcasted" researchers including Centauries. Each of these scientists and researchers was trying to prove their professional expertise, to surpass and outdo oneself. The results of their efforts exceeded all, even the wildest expectations. Moreover, the Enterprise actively financed scientific and industrial espionage.

As the result of all the efforts conducted, the work on "space engine" creation advanced very significantly. Furthermore, for the exploration of uninhabited planets and mining of rare and valuable metals that will be used for the engine, the Enterprise financed development of technology that would allow temporary micro climate formation, as well as invention of creatures that would possess some level of intelligence, and at the same time, be very stable not only at the extremes of temperature, but also in the absence, different composition, or scarce atmosphere. Notably, these creatures—Humanoids will be created to carry out specific targeted tasks. After completion of a certain task, they will be reprogrammed, their "brains" will be literally "re-tuned."

Doctor Warren Van Bright, a very talented, but not so successful in a casual sense scientist, came up with an idea of a "biological dome," that could be used in certain parts of the globe, where extremes of climate hamper human life-sustaining activity. He had synthesized and patented a substance by means of which, depending on the ambient, one could either absorb and enhance sun heat rays, or reflect them cooling it down. By his design, a capsule, containing the substance would be discharged to a certain predetermined height, where it will blow up and a chemical reaction, creating transparent weightless micro climate creating substance will take place. The micro climate created would extend to a certain, pre-determined territory and time. Although, in general, the idea of micro climate formation was not new, his particular project, implied additional chemical reactions that would allow a more controlled and smooth change of temperature depending on necessities, and furthermore, will initiate a reaction to produce and release molecular oxygen.

Nevertheless, his project has been rejected as too costly and unreal. He, however managed to publish his preliminary results in a scientific journal, and, surprisingly, soon received a notification from one of the private Pharmaceutical companies that they were interested in his project and were willing to finance it. The offer was very tempting and he agreed to collaborate with them.

Thus, the murder that occurred in the club house during the play; the case that at the beginning was not even taken seriously, and only on Doctor Van Bright's insistence received proper attention, turned out to be much broader than anybody could imagine. The crime solving work now was conducted conjointly with the FBI. Link-by-link, a criminal chain was piling up. A noticeable part was played by Steven's son, Brian, who meticulously followed clues, would not miss slightest details and picking up the trail would follow it as a tracker dog.

Considerable help was also rendered by Suzy, long time collaborating with authorities, and her inseparable Four plus Jannette, a squad, whereas, caught into the whirligig of events and suspecting nothing at the beginning, Judy, was constantly subjected to a serious danger.

31 JUDY AND ETIENNE GO TO BRAZIL

In spite of the incident in the club house and ongoing investigation, things in the clinic, as well as in the club house, were in the best way possible. Treatment results were impressive, patients improved, and Doctor Van Bright felt good about it.

Right after discussion of a new patient and ending of the morning conference, Doctor Van Bright invited Judy to his office. He inquired about her future plans and intentions regarding her mysterious medallion. The previous evening Etienne had phoned her from Paris. He had new information about the location of the building, a blueprint of what they had found on the island. His investigation showed that it was a functioning University, founded and funded by one of the Jesuit monks and located in Rio de Janeiro. He also mentioned that he was quite ready to undertake a journey now to Brazil. Judy mentioned all these to Doctor Van Bright and he suggested not to put off the matter, especially that due to circumstances it would be prudent for her to leave Los Angeles for a while. Judy readily agreed with him.

Finishing her work, Judy left the hospital. The same evening, she called Etienne in Paris and they made arrangements for their new journey, this time to Brazil.

She arrived at the airport well in advance, unhurriedly went through all the necessary safety procedures, and made herself comfortable at the departure area. She took a glance over gathering passengers of her flight and pulled out of her purse an interesting book to read. The plot seemed to be very captivating; she read testimonials and about the author. Her thoughts, however, were far from the story line, as they strayed around recent happenings such as the incident with Suzy and Manuel, the voyage on Roger's yacht and growing good feelings about him. She liked his respectful attitude towards crew members, his audacity, and ability to remain calm and put under any circumstances, not mentioning his professional experience and vast knowledge. Finding Centauries, accompanied by armed men on the island and his possible involvement with criminals, was also a head scratch giver. Most of all, however, she was excited by the anticipation of a possible prompt unveiling of her family secret. During her long flight, she believed, there would be enough time to finish the book.

"What's awaiting her in Brazil? Will they finally find the vanished collection?" Absorbed in her thoughts, Judy didn't notice as two strangers took their seats not far from her on either side, casting at her seemingly unintentional and absentminded glances from time to time.

The boarding, meantime, was underway and she joined the queue. In an orderly way, soon everybody was in the plane including the two strangers, who now happened to be with her in the same row.

The hours-long flight wound down safely and the airplane landed at the Rio de Janeiro airport. Judy claimed her luggage, rented a car, and drove up to the hotel where Etienne was already waiting for her.

They warmly met each other; both in anticipation of the possible near unveiling of their family mystery. They intended to visit the University the next morning and before that, just to get some rest.

The next morning, they met in the hotel's lobby and set out to the University in a rental car, taking with them the blueprint and, by experience, the icon found on the island. Thanks to footwork conducted by Etienne, including contacts with the University administration, they reached the place easily and were affably welcomed by their guide Señor Lucio, who intended to acquaint them with the University buildings, its history, and faculties.

Special attention was deserved for the multiple publications and works conducted in Astronomy. The University was also very proud of their observatory and one of their unique and spectacular halls, located in one of the up wings of the building. The hall was famous due to its construction and stained-glass windows that created its special lighting. The founder of the University, who was referred to as Father Bernard, wished to remain incognito. However, it was known that he joined the Jesuit Order, was very rich, and spent most of the time on one of the islands in the Caribbean Sea with his young friend Mongo, who had become as a son to him. Both of them shared a passion for stars and the Universe, and would spend hours by the telescope observing the starry sky and making their notes. However, by strange coincidences, their notes and workbooks vanished. Nevertheless, the University continues their tradition and constitutes one of the leaders in astronomical science.

Judy and Etienne showed the blueprint, they had found on the island to Señor Lucio.

"It's impossible," said Señor Lucio after carefully examining it.

"What is impossible?" in one voice surprised Judy and Etienne.

"I am sorry, but this is not correct." Judy and Etienne looked at each other.

"According to your blueprint there is hidden room under one of the up wings, exactly under the famous hall of World. I have known this building for long time and I never heard of any hidden rooms there, besides it doesn't correspond to the official blueprint, I can assure you." Driven by curiosity, they all hastily set forth to the hall. Judy and Etienne crossed the threshold of the hall and immediately were amazed by the sight. The lighting was really marvelous. The windows and colorful stained-glass windows were constructed in such a way that when the daylight goes through them the perception of the Aurora Borealis was created. In the middle of the hall on a low-level stand, a glittering globe was placed that reflected sun beams. The globe could be rotated if desired to view any part of the world. Continents and Oceans were well distinguishable, and they all started looking through them. The globe consisted of polished and closely fitted metal plates, which could be slid aside and back. Judy tried and easily moved several of them. In a certain position of the globe around its center line, the reflected lights from the globe come together in the center of a Gothic ceiling and created the perception of a beaming

144

star. She had never seen anything like this before and the idea flashed in her brain immediately —

"Northern Lights and the Polar star—correlate well with the name of Duke Orlofsky's jewelry collection and his famous diadem. Is this just a coincidence, or are they really on the right track?" Surprisingly, in this position of the globe at her fingertips happen to be North America and she slid aside the polished shining plate. There under the plate a deepening, resembling the shape of their medallion appeared. Without much reflection, simply by intuition, she removed the assembled medallion from her neck and placed it into the deepening. All of a sudden, the globe, along with the massive plate, they all stood on, started slowly lowering down. Judy and Etienne were set for possible hidden rooms and for this reason foreseeingly were armed with flashlights. All three of them found themselves in a tiny room, the huge part of which occupied the globe. Having already experience with hidden mechanisms, Judy and Etienne carefully inspected the walls of the room. They couldn't find anything particular besides a photograph on one of the walls. They took a good look at it. On the photograph, there was a building of quite an interesting design with what appeared to be an American flag in front of it. Judy took a picture of the photograph, put it back on the wall, and pulled the medallion from the deepening. The massive plate with the globe immediately started moving again and ascended them all back. Judy and Etienne thanked the stupefied Señor Lucio for his kind assistance, walked a little bit around the University campus and returned to the hotel.

What is it? A dead end? Is their search over? What relation has this building with the American flag in front of it to their matter?

One could assume that the building is located in the United States but what State, what city and does it have any relation to their enigma?

These questions were on the mind of both of them. The next day they departed to Los Angeles.

32 THE TABATIERE

Judy and Etienne returned to Los Angeles. Joseph, who accepted Roger's offer was looking for a suitable housing and temporarily lived at Judy's taking care of Kitty. On their return, they related to him everything about their trip and the finding. They also printed out the photograph of the picture found in the secret room.

Judy gave a call to Dr. Van Bright, announcing her return, and he invited her along with Joseph and Etienne to his villa. The next day they all headed to Dr. Van Bright's, where they met Steven and Brian. Everybody listened to Judy's relation about the trip with interest. She brought the print of the photograph with her. Doctor Van Bright took the print and started attentively examining it with a magnifying glass and then handed it to Steven.

"It sure looks like the building is right here in America, but what city?" pensively said Steven, iterating Judy's thoughts and handing the print to Brian. Brian simply glanced at it and without even a second look, announced--

"Oh, I know this building very well. I even had a chance to visit it once, although it is very seldom open for visitors."

Everybody literally froze in surprise. Sensing the impression his words made on everybody, Brian took a prolonged pause, triumphantly looked over them and pronounced-

"It's a snuffbox, they call it Tabatiere!"

"A snuffbox, Tabatiere?" surprised, everybody repeated his words in unison.

"Oh, yeah, mystery snuffbox or simply Tabatiere. This is a building well-known among collectors. As rumor has it, there are secret rooms and even hidden floors, still awaiting to be uncovered. The building was built in Philadelphia in the last century. It reminds one of a gigantic snuffboxes, and contains a famous museum of antiques."

Now everybody dashed to the print. It was clear, the building really reminded a gigantic snuff box.

"Does its roof open up as well?" calmly and quite seriously asked Joseph, intently observing his fogged tall glass, filled with bubbling soda.

"It's quite possible," immediately replied Brian. But you see the owners of the house are not eager to reveal its secrets. There were, of course, unauthorized attempts to do so, but so far to no avail. By the way," remarked Brien, "besides the interesting exposition, the salon has remarkable lightning carried out by antique crystal chandeliers and the chandeliers of colored glass, that create a twinkling effect. The most remarkable, from my point of view, is a ball, covered with thin metal plates, resembling a big globe."

A globe? Globe again? Judy and Etienne exchanged glances as if trying to say,

"Well, it looks now we are really close to revelation. All we need to do is go to Philadelphia, visit the famous salon, and open up that gigantic snuffbox with its secrets."

"I almost forgot, a research conference is going to be held in Philadelphia right next week; it'll be interesting for you to attend it, Judy," quite worthily remarked Doctor Van Bright.

"And we could all together visit the salon, or should I say the mysterious Tabatiere?"

Unbelievable, after all these trips and intertwinement the solution of the mystery could be right here under their fingertips.

Everything was unfolding really well. The trip to Philadelphia was scheduled for the next week. Brian, who had real passion for antiquity, especially antique furniture and mystery boxes, was very enthusiastic about the trip, especially now, when a vanished famous collection could be traced to this inscrutable building.

The party arrived in Philadelphia and checked into the hotel, where the research conference was taking place. Doctor Van Bright and Judy registered for the conference and everybody comfortably settled down in their suites. The next day after the conference, the party got together in the main lobby and set forth to the mysterious building in two rental cars. Judy was driving Joseph and Etienne, and Steven -- Doctor Van Bright and Brian.

It was end of the day and the traffic was really heavy. Nevertheless, both cars uneventfully reached a gray, four story stone building with column pillars and a wavering American flag at the entrance. They circled the building, which really resembled a gigantic antique snuff box, and found parking. A modest-sized park with its neatly manicured green lawn, and gray stone benches, the same as the building in front of it, created the impression of an ensemble. Judy and Etienne immediately noticed the benches, which strikingly resembled the benches in front of the cave in Paris. This, seemingly insignificant detail, also promised that they were very close to solving their mystery. The entrance was free, but, regretfully, the salon was closed to visitors. Nevertheless, in a few minutes in front of them an attendant appeared. Steven and Brian pulled out their badges and explained to him, without going into particulars and details, that they have a very special reason to visit the salon. The attendant listened to them very attentively and then asked them to wait a while. Meantime, he made a phone call and when he returned, opened the door and let them in. The party entered through main entrance, that amazingly resembled a key-hole. They immediately found themselves in a large hall, where antique furniture, and all kind of antiquity including paintings, arms, musical instruments, and household articles were displayed. The salon was lit up by crystal chandeliers and lusters of multicolored glass. The soft light they created enhanced the impression from the exquisite items displayed. One of the most remarkable displays was a cosmic exposition, where paintings, telescopes, and all kinds of antique instruments, previously used for cosmic research and measurements, were displayed. In the center of the cosmic exposition, on a low-level broad pedestal, a bow shaped rest held a large ball. Over the ball, as if be-girding it, two thin metal hoops overtopped, crossing over each other. The ball reminded Judy of the terrestrial globe with its engrained metal plates. By experience, Judy and Etienne immediately headed for the globe, and everybody followed them. They started attentively viewing it. Strangely, however, they couldn't find the customary outlines of oceans, seas, continents, and mainlands on the globe. Instead, thin metal plates were curved in a way that created strange extraterrestrial configurations with prominences, craters, and connecting canals. Judy noticed, that one of the "craters" remotely resembled their medallion. She tried the metal plate, but could not slide it aside. Since the plate wouldn't move aside, she raised it slightly over the globe. Under the plate there was another "crater" that exactly matched the shape of the medallion. She removed the medallion from her neck and placed it into the heart shaped "crater." After that, she closed the crater. In front of everybody's eyes, the globe came to life and slowly started turning about its axis. The most remarkable thing, however, was that turning of the globe created a feeling that the hoops are circling the globe, imitating the trajectory of celestial bodies. All of a sudden, the globe stopped and started opening up as a flower, whose petals were found to be in between hoops. Then, a remarkable sight made everyone hold their breath. Inside the globe, on a black velvet stand playing with all rainbow colors, a miracle piece of jewelry opened up. This was a tiara. The shiny inside surface of the globe enhanced the glowing of the precious stones. One of these stones stood out by its size and beauty, resembling a star by shape. It's hard to describe the admiration and joy they felt looking at it. The famous tiara known by the name of the diadem of Northern Lights, that gave name to the entire vanished jewelry collection of Duke Orlofsky, was glowing in front of them! Is it a dream? Neither Judy, nor Etienne could believe their eyes. Their medallion, the mysterious medallion, by some inscrutable ways brought together complete strangers living in different countries and continents, and, furthermore, led them to this remarkable building with its contents, secrets, puzzles, and the possible unveiling of their family secret, interwoven somehow with Duke Orlofsky and his rich jewelry collection.

However, their exuberance was replaced by astonishment when the entire pedestal, along with diadem, the globe and its hoops started sinking disappearing out of their sight. At the same time, the floor under their feet started to move. One of the slabs shifted, covering the space of the disappearing globe, and opening next to it, a staircase leading down. Judy, Etienne, Doctor Van Bright, Steven, Brian, and Joseph offhandedly started descending the stairs, and soon found themselves in a basement. Judy and Etienne, equipped with flashlights, lit the modest sized space and immediately noticed a narrow corridor. As a matter of fact, there were several of them and even a few stairs, leading up. Everybody hastened to one of the corridors. However, after walking some distance in the narrowing passage-way, they came against the wall and had to go back.

"Wait!" exclaimed Brian. "After all, this is a mystery snuff box, it's reflected in its name. Here, just as in any mystery box, everything is not so simple! It is obvious. This corridor, just like many others, is simply a wrong tack. There should be a secret 'pullout drawer,' which will allow us to move in the right direction."

"A 'pullout drawer,' what do you mean by that?"

"There should be a secret door," explained Brian. "Let's look for it without losing time," Brian confidently asserted approaching one of the walls and lighting it up with flashlight. Only now, Judy noticed one of the walls that was faced with small gray stones absolutely similar to ones they had found in the cave under Paris. She moved to the wall and leaned heavily on it. The wall gave way under the pressure, and started to move, swinging around and revealing behind it, as she had expected, a heavy door. Judy pulled out of her bag a big carved key, already known to everybody, which she always carried on her, calling it my "talisman." She inserted the key into the keyhole and turning it, opened the door. Behind the door there was a staircase. Everybody went inside the doorway and started ascending the staircase. After a few ladder landings they got the impression that they were on the third or fourth floor. Finally, the staircase brought them to a spacious hall. Thanks to the unique construction of the building, one could reach this hall only through the basement, as all the other approaches were encumbered with thick walls. In other words, this part of the building was completely isolated from others. The windows were draped with heavy curtains, nevertheless, the hall was lit and it was completely mystical where the light was coming from. On one of the walls was a large painting, that reached the floor, of a groom and a bride, wearing a tiara and other exquisite jewelry. On her neck, one could see the famous medallion. In the middle of the hall, on a pedestal with an opened "globe," the tiara was gleaming. On an antique desk, which immediately evoked Brian's attention, some papers were laid out. Brian, as an enthusiastic antiquarian with special interest to desks and mystery boxes, immediately started a thorough examination. No sooner had he pulled out a hidden drawer then the light in the hall started dimming down and the hall plunged into complete darkness. At the same time, the ceiling started to slide apart and twinkling stars and a shiny moon appeared over their heads. It felt like one of the distant Galaxies had started drawing closer and one could clearly distinguish in it two bright stars, one of them slightly larger than the other. Most amazingly, circling around these stars appeared a celestial body, resembling a planet. Joseph became very excited:

"It looks like a Centauries constellation and these bright stars are Centauries A and B, that could be observed from the Southern Hemisphere, specifically from Brazil, as you visited just recently!" He said.

They didn't notice immediately when around the tiara, lights appeared and it started gleaming as the Northern Lights, a symbolic unity of North and South. Everybody was so absorbed with the ceiling, that nobody noticed what was going on under their feet.

"Look!" Everybody heard Brian's excited voice, and all eyes swayed at him. Following his gaze, they became stunned by the sight. The wall with the portrait disappeared and instead a continuance of the Universe with twinkling stars was all around them. Almost a head-spinning perception came over them of being an integral part of this Universe, but just a grain in this formidable ocean of stars. Wonder-struck and mesmerized by the sight, they couldn't utter a word.

Gradually, the starry sky withered away and ultimately completely vanished. At the same time, the hall was becoming lighter. The wall with the portrait miraculously reappeared. Everybody curiously approached the portrait and now tried to move it. The portrait easily turned around opening behind it an entrance. They all entered a large room. What they saw there exceeded all, even the wildest, expectations. On the tables and cabinets with dark colored velvet, and covered with glass, there were placed precious and semiprecious stones, imitating the shape and colors of distant galaxies. Separately displayed were exceptionally beautiful and expensive fine pieces of jewelry. Carried away by viewing the exposition, nobody noticed someone appearing behind their backs.

As Judy so Etienne, visiting the Tabatiere, needless to say, hoped to solve their mystery, nonetheless, what they were observing exceeded all their expectations: sparkling precious and semiprecious stones laid out as fantastic distant galaxies, expensive fine jewelry made of silver, gold, and platinum, including boxes and jewel cases, that would take Brian's breath away, and many more. Speechless with occasional excited outcries, they moved from one exposition to another.

Suddenly a slight cough broke the silence and everybody looked in that direction. An unknown tall man with somewhat coarse but, nevertheless, pleasant features of about 30-40 years of age was observing the excited attendees. His black clothes enhanced his stately athletic body type. Nobody had noticed when he had appeared. The man approached the group.

"Messrs.' welcome to my house, my name is Theodore." Everybody immediately repaid the salutation. He was holding in his hands a wooden box, made in the shape of a coffer, with a large, out of proportion, keyhole. On seeing the coffer, which turned out to be an exact copy of her grandmother's ancient trunk, Judy immediately pulled out her famous inlaid key, that had already opened several hidden doors.

"I believe, then, this belongs to you," said Theodore, noticing the key, and he handed the coffer over to her. Judy gingerly took the coffer and put it down on one of the tables. She inserted her key into the keyhole and opened it easily. The dark green velvet upholstered coffer contained books in a brown leather binding, that turned out to be a diary, where Duke Orlofsky had described his life's journey; his will, instructions, and arrangements in favor of his son and daughter and their descendants. In the will, he also mentioned his friend Mongo and his descendants.

152

Theodore, who himself didn't know what exactly was hidden in the building, called Tabatiere with secret, in which he had lived since his birth, invited the amazed visitors to his chamber to celebrate the occasion and tell something about himself.

As it turned out, the owner of the building and the antiquity salon was the great grandson of Duke Orlofsky's young friend Mongo to whom the Duke trusted his collection after his death. Mongo's descendants inherited the building and the antiquity salon, except for the contents of the hidden rooms. He gave Mongo exact instructions what to do when the true inheritors of the hidden rooms would appear. Nobody, however, knew where these hidden rooms were located, as they didn't have the blueprint. Mongo's descendants sharply honored all the Duke's instructions and were rewarded for this with considerable means.

33 THE DIARY OF THE DUKE
AND THE EPILOGUE

The diaries of Duke Orlofsky found in the box explained a great deal. In his diary, he colorfully and in details described the developments with his marriage, estrangement with his dearly beloved folks, and exile to Caucasus. Sweeping through the country revolution, post-revolutionary terror, and bloodshed forced him to leave the country. He managed to move to France and take his son to safety, and, subsequently, move his entire collection. Of great assistance to him were Georgian monks, who concealed him in a hidden monastic cell. The Duke kept his hopes up that the political situation in the country would improve, his daughter would recover, and that his family reunite again. However, fate made disposition otherwise, and his hopes were answered only partially.

For the purpose of security and due to his beliefs, Duke Orlofsky joined the Jesuit Order and, leaving behind his son under assumed French name in one of the monasteries near Paris, left for Brazil.

He also managed under the NKVD (People's Commissariat for Internal Affairs) very nose to carry out his famous and richest jewelry collection to Brazil. Under the name Farther Bernard, the Duke had returned to France several times and, without revealing his kinship, safeguarded his son's support and education. He also gave him the medallion when he came to age. Making inquiries about his daughter, who remained in Russia, that time was extremely dangerous, nevertheless, he learned that she overcame her illness and recovered.

In Brazil, Duke Orlofsky profitably invested his funds and grew even richer. On top of that, explorations undertaken with the brothers De Sanchez increased his wealth significantly.

During his dangerous journey in the Brazilian rainforests, he met a young Indian by the name Mongo, who saved the Duke's life pulling him out of churning water. The Duke, in his turn, paid for Mongo's education, and cured him from severe malaria which he contracted during one of his recurrent returns to rainforests. A strong longstanding friendship arose between them, which was also bolstered by their mutual passion for Astronomy.

The Duke confounded and co funded the University in Rio de Janeiro, that functions to this day, and significantly contributes to astronomical research. Analysis and calculations conducted at the University indicated the possible existence of a celestial body, a planet, or more precisely, a binary system similar to Earth—Moon. Although their trajectories were calculated, they couldn't detect them. The best place for observation over the system, as they contemplated, was an island in the Caribbean Sea, where they built an observatory. After several years of persistent observations, the Duke and Mongo were able to see the planet and put it on an astronomical map. The characteristics of a new planet, due to its location in the solar system indicated that it could be similar to Earth.

However, volcanic eruption that took place on the island ruined the island along with their plans and they had to abandon it without detecting the satellite of a new planet.

Father Bernard and Mongo decided to move to the United States. Troubling news from Russia, the persecution of Russian emigres, and the necessity to maintain severe conspiracy contributed great deal to their decision.

In the United States they built a building named Tabatiere with secret and here-into moved safely the jewelry collection to which Soviet government manifested unfailing interest.

During one of his voyages to the islands in the Caribbean Sea, which he undertook regularly with Mongo, the Duke caught pneumonia and shortly perished. Nevertheless, before dying, sensing his failing health he settled his affairs. After the Duke's death, Mongo became custodian of his assets. In his will, the Duke equally mentioned his son and daughter as well as all Maria's children. He also mentioned Mongo and his descendants.

His entire cosmic exposition with precious and semiprecious stones including the famous diadem Northern Lights and the Polar Star diamond, he donated to the American National Museum.

The son and the daughter of Duke, brother and sister, separated in early childhood and by the will of fate found to be in different countries, never suspected of each other's existence, or of their true ancestry. Their descendants-- Judy and Etienne, were brought together by merely a matter of chance. The high-skilled medallion of a rare construction and beauty, created by the Duke himself and presented to his bride, played a decisive part. Hence, the striking similarity in appearance between Judy and Etienne turned out to be not simply coincidental, but caused by their kinship.

As per calculations of Centauries, an amateur astronomer, there should be a planet in the Solar system where conditions could be similar to Earth due to its special location. The best observation site for the planet would be on the island in the Caribbean Sea. Here the calculations conducted by the Duke and Centauries coincided. At the same time, ambitious plans of the criminal syndicate included instituting their control on Earth as well as in Space by cosmic piracy. They contemplated reclamation of one of the planets in the Solar system as well, by changing its climate and making it inhabitable for humans. As it was mentioned above, for these reasons the criminal syndicate financed technology developments and actively was engaged in sci-tech espionage.

Thus, the Police investigation of a murder and its motives that presumably occurred in the club house during the play, and disappearance of the statue of the innocent Farmers Bear Billy, that at the beginning seemed as something out of fantasy, suddenly acquired completely new outlines and led them to sci-tech espionage and movement of a large consignment of drugs. The FBI, in its turn, followed the drug traffickers foot-steps long before and managed to plant undercover agents and informers into the criminal chain. Suzy, besides her participation in the medical research study collaborated with the FBI and wound up in Los Angeles along with her old friend and accomplice, Napoleon. The participation of Suzy and her squad drawn by her into this business turned out to be very fruitful. They actively "drew the fire" on themselves and as a consequence Suzy and Judy were kidnapped and met Manuel. The surprising encounter of Manuel in the company of Centauries on the island will link together two criminal activities of the syndicate—spreading the drugs and sci-tech espionage that served their purpose to establish control over the Earth by cosmic piracy.

Hence, an accidental intersection of Judy and Centauries on the island will play a crucial part in cracking of the entire criminal scheme—drugs, sci-tech espionage, and far-reaching cosmic plans of ambitious criminal lords.

The matter, thus, turned out to be much broader than anybody could imagine at first. It is also necessary to say, that a close satellite observation over the afore-mentioned islands immediately commenced and the "research" expedition to the region was contemplated.

Unsuspecting and without a clue at the beginning, Judy, who was caught into the whirl of activity, finally was amply rewarded for her persistent search and unraveling her family mystery.